"I Can't Just Hop Into Bed With You Because You Turn Me On," Madeline Said.

"If it's what we both want, why not?" Chase countered.

"Because there are other things that need to be taken into consideration."

"Like what?"

"Like the fact that we have to work together. And then there's my father. He—"

"Leave your father out of this, Madeline. What's between us has nothing to do with him," Chase said, his voice hard, his eyes even harder. "This has to do with you and me. It has to do with sex. My wanting you and you wanting me."

* * *

"New author Metsy Hingle has the talent...the originality, to imbue new life on a very old human emotion, making this work a beautiful love story. Believable yet magical. 4+"
—Harriet Klausner, *Affaire de Coeur*

Dear Reader,

Established stars and exciting new names...that's what's in store for you this month from Silhouette Desire. Let's begin with Cait London's MAN OF THE MONTH, *Tallchief's Bride*—it's also the latest in her wonderful series, THE TALLCHIEFS.

The fun continues with *Babies by the Busload,* the next book in Raye Morgan's THE BABY SHOWER series, and *Michael's Baby,* the first installment of Cathie Linz's delightful series, THREE WEDDINGS AND A GIFT.

So many of you have indicated how much you love the work of Peggy Moreland, so I know you'll all be excited about her latest sensuous romp, *A Willful Marriage.* And Anne Eames, who made her debut earlier in the year in Silhouette Desire's Celebration 1000, gives us more pleasure with *You're What?!* And if you enjoy a little melodrama with your romance, take a peek at Metsy Hingle's enthralling new book, *Backfire.*

As always, each and every Silhouette Desire is sensuous, emotional and sure to leave you feeling good at the end of the day!

Happy Reading!

Lucia Macro

Senior Editor

Please address questions and book requests to:
Silhouette Reader Service
U.S.: 3010 Walden Ave., P.O. Box 1325, Buffalo, NY 14269
Canadian: P.O. Box 609, Fort Erie, Ont. L2A 5X3

METSY
HINGLE
BACKFIRE

SILHOUETTE *Desire*

Published by Silhouette Books

America's Publisher of Contemporary Romance

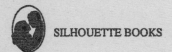 SILHOUETTE BOOKS

ISBN 0-373-76026-4

BACKFIRE

Copyright © 1996 by Metsy Hingle

Books by Metsy Hingle

Silhouette Desire

Seduced #900
Surrender #978
Backfire #1026

METSY HINGLE

is a native of New Orleans who loves the city in which she grew up. She credits the charm, antiquity and decadence of her birthplace, along with the passionate nature of her own French heritage, with instilling in her the desire to write. Married and the mother of four children, she believes in romance and happy endings. Becoming a Silhouette author is a long-cherished dream come true for Metsy and one happy ending that she continues to celebrate with each new story she writes.

For Linda Hayes—
My agent and friend, with thanks
for encouraging me to shoot for the stars and then
helping me to reach them.

Prologue

The branches of the big oak tree swayed under the rush of wind. Chase McAllister pressed his hand against the window, feeling the cold December air seep through the glass and chill his fingertips. He looked at the little white lights that the brothers at St. Mark's Home for Boys had strung through the tree's branches for Christmas.

One. Two. Three. Four. He began counting the lights. Counting the lights was more fun than watching the other kids getting all mushy with their families. He didn't want to see them climb into the cars and drive away to spend the Christmas holidays with their moms or dads or grandparents. He didn't want to think about how there wasn't anyone coming for him.

Five. Six. Seven. Eight.

Chase's gaze drifted to the big white car that Billy Taylor was getting into. The woman inside pulled Billy to her and hugged him to her chest. Chase looked away. He rubbed at his eyes, feeling that sting behind them again. He wasn't going to cry, Chase told himself. Crying was for babies. And he wasn't a baby anymore. He was eight years old. A "little man." That's what his mother had called him. And men didn't cry.

"Poor little tyke. Guess he'll have to stay here at the big house for Christmas."

Catching the reflections of the housekeeper and her new assistant in the window, Chase swiped at his eyes again. Go away, he ordered silently, willing them to leave. He didn't want to talk to them. He didn't want to talk to anyone.

"But I thought you said all the boys got to go home for Christmas," the new housekeeper said. "How come he don't?"

"'Cause he ain't got no place to go. His momma killed herself, and he ain't got no daddy—at least none that claims him. Surely you heard the story," the older woman said, her voice dropping to a whisper.

Ignoring the two women, Chase watched the car with Billy in it drive off down the street. He swallowed. He wasn't going to cry, he reminded himself, feeling that achiness in his chest again. He was never, ever going to cry again.

Fingering the scar along his chin, he went back to counting the lights.

Nine. Ten. Eleven . . .

One

The place hadn't changed much, Chase thought as he studied the garden room of the Saint Charles Hotel from his position near the dais. The cloths covering the tables were still made of pink damask and, given their faded appearance, he would lay odds they were the same ones that had covered the tables twenty-six years ago. The fresh flowers on the tables were fewer in number, but the vases holding them were genuine crystal.

Surveying the crowd of reporters and local bigwigs, who had gathered for the formal announcement of the new partnership between his firm and Henri Charbonnet, Chase frowned. Even the faces and names looked the same, he thought, recalling those Sunday mornings his mother had spent scouring the newspaper's society pages and pointing out her customers to him. The crème de la crème of New Orleans, she had called them. He doubted that any of them had even known the name of the pretty waitress who had served them their coffee and five-course meals. But she had known *their* names. She had idolized them, had been thrilled to touch the fringes of their pampered lives.

And now they were here to see him.

Of course, their eagerness to welcome him into their privileged midst was due to his alignment with one of their own—Henri Charbonnet.

Chase shifted his gaze to the object of his thoughts. The years had not been as kind to Henri Charbonnet as they had been to his hotel. The man's hair was thinner now and nearly all white. His middle had thickened, giving him a portly appearance. He had loomed as a giant in the memory of an eight-year-old boy, but now he appeared almost short against Chase's own six feet. But the eyes…those hard green eyes that had been so cold and forbidding when they had stared at him from across his mother's coffin…they hadn't changed. They were just as cold, just as empty, just as unfeeling as he remembered.

Henri Charbonnet shook hands with one of the city's councilmen, then tipped his head back in laughter before leading a group of his friends to one of the serving stations. The hotel's finest crystal and silver pieces adorned the tables laden with the restaurant's signature dishes.

Charbonnet had spared little expense for the press briefing and reception that was to follow, Chase surmised, as he took in the lavishly decorated room. Evidently cost didn't matter to the man when it was someone else's money he was spending. Chase gritted his teeth and rubbed his thumb across the two-inch scar that stretched across his chin. Enjoy your little kingdom while you can, old man, he thought. Because it won't be yours for much longer.

Chase shifted his gaze to the doorway where the guests continued to filter into the room at a steady pace.

Then he saw the brunette.

Despite her small size, she was a hard one to miss in that red suit. The fabric skimmed nicely rounded curves and fell several inches above her knees on legs that seemed impossibly long for a woman who couldn't measure more than five foot four.

Nice, Chase thought. He appreciated the female form as much as the next man. And while he had never been a man who got overly excited by big-breasted women, legs were another story.

Chase smiled as he took another look at hers. The brunette definitely had a great pair of legs. Slowly, Chase inched his gaze upward from the expensive red pumps to the mouth painted the same shade of cherry red as her suit. A mouth made for kissing, he thought idly.

The rest of her face wasn't bad, either. She wasn't beautiful, at least not by movie-star standards, but she was pretty all the same. She greeted several people and seemed to scan the crowd in search of someone. With her face turned to the side, he couldn't quite make out if her eyes were green or blue. The thick cocoa-colored hair fell in a smooth and chic line just below her chin and was a great foil for her skin. Ah, and what skin, Chase thought as he studied her. The color of rich cream, it looked as soft and delicate as the petal of a rose.

An expensive rose, Chase decided, catching the flicker of diamond studs when she tucked a strand of hair behind one ear. She smiled at something the pretty boy in the Italian suit said, her luscious mouth curving up sweetly at the other man.

She's out of your league, McAllister, a voice inside him taunted. This rose was one sweet, tempting little package with all the class and breeding her daddy's money could buy. And no doubt if she hadn't yet landed herself a rich husband to pick up where daddy left off, she soon would.

"Mr. McAllister." One of the newspaper reporters approached him and introduced herself. The smile the woman gave him reminded him of a cat, a big hungry cat. "I know you can't divulge the details of your firm's purchase of stock in the Saint Charles, but can you tell me if it's true that Majestic Hotels plans to invest several million dollars in the renovation of the hotel?"

So the rumor mill was already buzzing. "My firm plans to invest a considerable amount of money in renovating the property," he said, favoring her with one of his lazy smiles. Using his smile to charm others had been one of the first tricks he had learned in the foster home circuit, and it had served him well in the hotel business. People liked dealing with a person who smiled. And women especially seemed to like his. "But how much the renovation is going to cost has yet to be determined," he said noncommittally.

Out of the corner of his eye, Chase watched his expensive rose weave her way through the crowd with the pretty boy in tow to where Henri Charbonnet and his group stood. She greeted him and several of those gathered with a kiss on the cheek in the fashion so typical of Southern women.

"What about the actual running of the hotel? Word has it that Majestic likes to bring in their own general managers. Is that why you're here? Do you plan to take over as the new general manager of the Saint Charles?"

Chase pulled his attention back to the reporter. His assessment of the woman as a cat was evidently on target, he decided. And from the hungry gleam in her eye, this one probably had sharp claws. Evidently she smelled another story behind Charbonnet's decision to sell an interest in the family's legacy to an outsider.

But it was a story he had no interest in telling. He had his own agenda where Charbonnet was concerned and had no intention of meeting someone else's...no matter how tempting. "Now, Bitsy," he said, addressing her by the first name printed on her name tag. "Whatever gave you that idea?"

"Oh, just a hunch." She gave him an assessing look and Chase suspected she liked what she saw. "But I can see you're not going to tell me anything more. So what's the official line on your involvement here?"

He gave the woman his best smile and watched it take effect. "My role at the Saint Charles will be to oversee the implementation of new reporting and reservation systems, linking the hotel with Majestic's mother systems. And I'll also be working to get the renovations under way."

"And Henri Charbonnet's role?"

"Henri Charbonnet is the hotel's executive director, as well as one of its owners. But I suspect you already know that. Majestic plans to work very closely with him in the operation of the Saint Charles."

"What about his daughter, Madeline?"

"What about her?" Chase tossed back, resisting the urge to check on his rose.

The reporter cut a glance to Henri Charbonnet, then looked back at him. A thin smile spread across the reporter's lips. "Well, I understand Madeline wasn't very happy about her father's decision to sell an interest in the hotel...that she had hoped to take over the operation of the Saint Charles herself someday," the woman continued. "I was just wondering if you or Majestic Hotels saw Madeline's position at the hotel as a problem."

He had given little thought to Madeline Charbonnet when he had been making his plans. He had noted her name on the list of the sales department's employees and dismissed it. He assumed she was one of the reasons the place was operating in the red. The fact that she had not attended the staff meeting he had held the previous day and had been missing from the sales department—on vacation they said— had confirmed his opinion of her as a spoiled little rich girl playing at the hotel business. If the daughter was anything like her father, she would have only contributed to the financial drain. He had simply added her name to the list of problems at the hotel that he would need to fix. Of course, he had no intention of telling the reporter that. Instead, he simply replied, "I don't see Madeline Charbonnet as a problem at all."

Excusing himself from the reporter, Chase headed in Charbonnet's direction. He told himself he simply wanted to get this dog-and-pony show on the road, that it had nothing to do with the brunette standing beside the older man. Stopping just behind Charbonnet, Chase waited for him to finish his conversation before suggesting they get the statements to the press out of the way. And he used the moment to study the brunette.

Damn if that skin of hers didn't look even softer close up, he thought. Even her voice matched. It was all velvety and soft as she made plans to meet pretty boy for breakfast the next morning. Unable to resist, Chase gave her legs another once-over. Definitely roses. The long-stemmed expensive variety.

"McAllister." Charbonnet stuck out his hand, motioning for Chase to join him. He made quick introductions of the men, then turned to the brunette. "And I don't believe you've met my daughter, Madeline. Madeline, this is Chase McAllister with Majestic Hotels."

He should have seen that one coming, Chase admonished himself. Quickly, he schooled his expression, looking at Madeline Charbonnet more closely.

The black-and-white newspaper photographs he had seen of her through the years—clips of her as a debutante, a maid for the old-line carnival clubs and society darling—none had done justice to the woman who stood before him. They hadn't revealed that the lips now pressed together in a tight line were so full and sensuous or that the eyes set in that perfect oval face were such a deep green. The newspaper photographs certainly hadn't prepared him for the fact that those green eyes would be a mirror of everything she was feeling.

And right now, judging from the fire flashing in those emerald gems, Chase had no doubt that Madeline Charbonnet would like nothing better than to deck him.

The thought amused him and Chase smiled, which only seemed to make those eyes of hers grow even darker. But he had to give her credit because instead of slugging him, she extended her hand. "Mr. McAllister," she said, her voice as cool as the February wind that whipped at the flags flying outside of the hotel.

Chase bit back the urge to laugh at the regal tilt of her chin. "Ms. Charbonnet. It's a pleasure. And please, call me Chase." Damn if her skin wasn't every bit as silky and soft as he had imagined. She even smelled like roses.

And no doubt she came with her own supply of thorns, a voice inside Chase warned. Before he could dwell on that thought further, the ear-piercing shrill of a microphone being flipped on sliced through the room.

Madeline pulled her hand free. She took a step back, then turned to Charbonnet. "Father, I believe they're ready for you and Mr. McAllister to take your positions at the podium," she told him.

"Would you like to join your father and me at the podium for the announcement?" Chase asked.

"No." Madeline's faced flushed an angry red. "Thank you, but no. The Saint Charles belongs to my father and . . . and to Majestic Hotels."

"I know. But you're still welcome—"

"Mr. McAllister, I don't *want* to join you and my father at the podium. If it had been my decision, there would be no need for an announcement today."

"Madeline, that's enough," Henri Charbonnet said firmly.

So the reporter had been right. Madeline Charbonnet hadn't been happy about her father's decision to sell. In fact, she was out-and-out furious.

"Madeline, apologize to Mr. McAllister for your rudeness," Henri ordered.

Madeline looked as though her father had slapped her. She tipped up her chin. "I have nothing to apologize for. Mr. McAllister and his firm have no right to own a part of the Saint Charles. It belongs—"

"Madeline Claire—"

Chase touched the other man's shoulder. "Forget it, Charbonnet. It doesn't matter." Guilt prickled at Chase momentarily, but he pushed it aside. Charbonnet was the one who had robbed her of her legacy. Not him. He had merely supplied the means. The fact that the deal would serve his own purposes didn't matter. Ignoring the shimmer of tears in her eyes, Chase hardened his heart. "Then I guess it's fortunate for Majestic Hotels and me that the decision to sell the Saint Charles wasn't yours to make."

Turning away from Madeline, he motioned to her father. "Come on, Charbonnet. Let's get this thing over with." Without waiting for a reply, Chase strode to the front of the room.

As Charbonnet stepped up to the microphone, Chase move to the side and half listened while he announced the new partnership and outlined his grand plans for the hotel.

"As all of you know, the Saint Charles Hotel has always prided itself on its old-world elegance and its fine service. With Majestic Hotels as our new partner, we intend to not only uphold that tradition, but to expand upon it," Charbonnet continued. "Our guests will continue to enjoy all of the amenities now offered, plus some additional ones . . ."

Yes, the man was really good at spending money, Chase thought, confirming his earlier assessment. In this case, someone else's. But he would let the old man have his day, enjoy himself while he could. Because within six months, if all went as planned, Charbonnet's little kingdom would come crumbling down.

And what about Madeline Charbonnet?

She wasn't his problem. He had waited a long time for this moment. It was the culmination of years of working, watching and waiting. At last the vengeance he had sought was within his grasp.

He didn't intend to lose the chance to even the score simply because some spoiled little rich girl had starry-eyed notions about the hotel. Only a fool would fall for that "heart in her eyes" trick.

Yet as he looked down into the gathering where she listened to her father ramble on about the hotel's heritage and its long ties to the Charbonnet family, the pride and longing on that expressive face of hers looked real.

And as Henri Charbonnet introduced him, the flicker of betrayal and then anger that raced across her features before she turned and started for the exit didn't seem at all like a trick.

Forget about her, McAllister, Chase told himself as he stepped up to the microphone. "Ladies and gentlemen,

Honorable Mayor, members of the city council, distinguished guests and friends, on behalf of Majestic Hotels, I would like to take this opportunity to thank you . . ."

Madeline allowed the cool water from the faucet to run over her hands and wrists while she struggled to regain control of herself. After several long moments she reached over and turned off the tap.

What a foolish thing to do, Madeline told her image in the gilt-edged mirror that hung over the basin in the ladies' powder room. Not foolish, it was plain stupid, she amended. Color flooded her cheeks as she relived the frustration and anger she had experienced at Chase McAllister's cutting reply.

What angered her most was that he had been right—the decision to sell an interest in the hotel hadn't been hers. She had had absolutely no say in the matter. True, the hotel didn't belong to her. It belonged to her father. But she loved the place, had practically grown up in it. She knew every piece of furniture, every antique that filled each of the hotel's eighty suites. It was more than just a hotel, more than just a piece of real estate. It was her home. And the thought of strangers owning a part of it galled her, made her physically ill.

Drying her hands on the linen towels that bore the hotel's entwined letters S and C, Madeline tossed it into the brass container designated for soiled linens. She leaned against the marble countertop and squeezed her eyes shut.

But there wasn't a thing she could do about it. Not now. It was too late. And any hopes that she might have harbored of one day running the hotel were finished. Even if she could have eventually convinced her father that she was capable of running the Saint Charles, it no longer mattered. The decision would no longer be his. It belonged to some unknown board of directors on the East Coast who wouldn't care about the hotel's history or the fact that a Charbonnet had always been at its helm.

If only her father had given her a chance, confided in her. Maybe she could have helped him work out the financial problems without resorting to selling off a part of the hotel.

But he hadn't. He hadn't even bothered to discuss his problems or his decision to sell with her until it was too late. The realization made her angry, but more than that, it hurt. Because it just drove home what she already knew: in her father's eyes she could never measure up. If she had, he would never have opted to sell.

Biting back a sigh of frustration, Madeline opened her eyes. No matter how hard she worked, no matter how good she was at her job, her father didn't think she was capable of running the hotel. And now with Chase McAllister in the picture, she would never have the chance to prove him wrong.

At the thought of Chase McAllister, Madeline straightened. The man had unnerved her. She had been all too aware of him watching her. He had reminded her of a wolf, running his eyes over her lazily, as though he were contemplating taking a taste. Madeline shivered at the image of Chase's mouth on her skin. She smoothed her fingers down the sides of her skirt as she recalled the feel of his palm, strong and hard against her own, when she had offered him her hand.

Hard. It was a good word to describe Chase McAllister. Despite the heartbreaker smile that told her he knew just what effect he had on women, there had been something hot and dangerous in his eyes when her father had introduced them. While working with a man like him might prove exciting, it would be unsettling.

Not that she was likely to have to worry about *that* problem. Madeline stifled a groan. After her remarks today, she doubted he would keep her on the hotel's staff. She probably should just resign and get it over with. She was good at her job. She could hire on at one of the other hotels in the city. Heaven knew there were enough of them, new ones popping up like crazy since the opening of the casino. That's why she had arranged to meet Kyle for breakfast, to ask for his help.

But the thought of working anyplace else made her want to weep. She loved the Saint Charles. It was in her blood. The hotel...the people, they were like family. She hated the thought of leaving. How could she just walk away?

Why should she have to? The stubborn voice inside her asked. She had more right to be here than Chase McAllister did. Why should she make it easy for him and his firm to take over her family's hotel?

She wouldn't, Madeline vowed. Not without a fight. She wasn't going to quit. She wasn't going to run away and hide. If Chase McAllister wanted her out, then he was going to have to fire her. Tipping up her chin, she slipped the strap of her purse over her shoulder and headed back into the garden room where McAllister was speaking.

"Majestic Hotels is pleased to add the venerable Saint Charles Hotel to its family of fine, luxury properties..."

At the rear of the room, Madeline listened to Chase deliver his speech in that deep, authoritative voice of his. The fact that he had memorized his remarks and not used any notes was a nice touch, she conceded. So was that devilish smile that he kept flashing at the audience. From the looks on peoples' faces—particularly the female ones—it was working.

"...and who better to have as our partner than Henri Charbonnet, the gentleman whose family founded the hotel. I'm personally looking forward to working with Henri—" His amused gaze swept over the crowd and halted when he reached her. He paused, staring at her long moments. "And with his daughter Madeline."

Madeline glared at him. He was lying through his pretty white teeth and she knew it.

As though he could read her thoughts, Chase smiled at her then. His mouth curved in the most wicked smile. It was warm and deep, intimate, the type of knowing smile a man might share with his lover. The effect was delectable, captivating...and disturbing.

"Handsome fellow, isn't he?"

Madeline swung her gaze to the pregnant woman standing beside her. Chloe James. Friends all of their lives, Chloe was the closest thing to a sister she had. Chloe had always been the adventuresome one of the two, and right now Madeline didn't trust the silly grin pasted on her face. "Chloe, I didn't see you standing there."

"Yes. I know. You were too busy drooling over the hunk."

"I'm not going to even dignify that with a denial."

Ignoring her, Chloe went on, "Not that I blame you now. He really is good-looking, and that smile. Lord, it's enough to make a girl's knees go weak. The man certainly is sexy. Don't you agree?"

"If you like his type," Madeline replied as nonchalantly as she could. Not for the life of her would she admit that her own stomach had done a flip-flop before she had reminded herself just who he was.

The other woman chuckled. "Madeline, darling, regardless of what your type is, a woman would have to be dead not to notice a man like him."

Madeline arched her brow at her friend. "Need I remind you that you're a married woman, Chloe James? And a pregnant one at that? I wonder what Paul would have to say if he heard you?"

Chloe wrinkled her pert nose at Madeline. "Lighten up, Maddie. I didn't say I was going to take him home with me—not that I wouldn't be tempted to. I'm just saying he's easy on the eyes. You have to admit he's a lot different from the sort of fellows we used to date."

He *was* different from the men she usually dated, Madeline admitted. For one thing, Chase McAllister didn't have her ex-fiancé's polished good looks. Chase's dark blond hair was a tad too long, brushing the collar of his shirt, to be fashionable. His bone structure was good, and he certainly knew how to fill out a suit. But his skin was too deeply tanned for a man who supposedly spent his days behind a desk. And while his mouth curved into the most enticing smile, the scar that slashed across his chin ruined any chance of him being considered handsome—at least not in a conventional way.

"There's something about him," Chloe said. "Sort of... untamed. Makes a girl wonder what he'd be like in bed."

"Chloe!"

"Oh, all right. I'll shut up. But you have to admit he is sexy. Especially when he smiles."

And he certainly knew how to use that smile, Madeline decided, watching him charm the guests.

Chloe sighed. "You're lucky. You get to work side by side with him."

"Funny, but I don't think of myself as lucky at all."

Chloe's expression sobered. "I'm sorry, Madeline. I guess I wasn't thinking. I know how much you loved this place."

"I still love it." Madeline shrugged. "Don't pay any attention to me. It's not like my father sold out completely. At least I still get to work here." That is, if she still had a job in the morning.

"Now, ladies and gentlemen, please enjoy yourselves," her father said after Chase had turned the microphone back over to him. "Eat, drink and enjoy."

Ten minutes later Madeline set aside her untouched glass of champagne and started to work her way toward the exit. Her head was pounding, and if she had to keep the smile plastered on her face a moment longer, she was afraid her muscles would lock in the position permanently.

"If you want people to really believe you're happy about this merger, you're going to have to do better than that tight little smile you've been wearing."

Madeline whirled around, nearly knocking the champagne glass out of Chase's hand. She hadn't even heard him come up behind her. The realization unsettled her...almost as much as the man himself. "I'm not happy about the merger, Mr. McAllister. So, why should I pretend that I am?"

"Because it's important to your father that people not know the real reason he sold an interest in the hotel."

It was true. Her father had told everyone that Chase's firm had approached him, offering him a ridiculous sum of money for an interest in the hotel. He had claimed the deal had been too good to turn down—especially when he would remain at the helm of the hotel. He had bragged how he would use someone else's money to renovate the Saint Charles and increase his investment at the same time. But the truth was he wouldn't have been able to keep the hotel open for much longer without the influx of cash from Chase's firm. From what her father had finally told her, the bills had been piling up for months. Not that she would admit that to Chase. Changing the subject, she asked, "What's wrong with my smile?"

"It's as phony as a three-dollar bill."

"You mean like yours?" she tossed back.

Chase laughed, making deep grooves in his lean cheeks. And Madeline felt her stomach quiver in response. How could she abhor this man and find him attractive at the same time?

"No. Mine's much better. I've got the phony smile down to an art. Part of my upbringing, you might say. Most people can't tell the difference."

But she could. She had known right away when he had smiled at her that it was genuine, not that fake curving of his lips that he had used to charm the audience. But the smile had been far too intimate, and filled with a sexual interest that had left her breathless. "No doubt I'll get better."

"Not likely. Unless you can do something about those eyes."

"What's wrong with my eyes?" she demanded.

"Not a thing. They're quite beautiful, in fact. Your best feature... aside from your skin. You've got the most incredible skin, Madeline Charbonnet."

Madeline flushed. The air in her lungs seemed to grow shallow as his gaze skimmed over her. It was happening again. He hadn't laid a finger on her, just looked at her.

And yet her body tingled as though he had caressed her. Suddenly feeling vulnerable, she demanded, "So, what do my eyes have to do with perfecting the art of the 'phony smile' as you called it?"

"Everything. Yours are much too expressive." He took a step closer, bringing them almost toe-to-toe. Madeline forced herself to hold his gaze and not to step back. She refused to give him the satisfaction of knowing how much his nearness unnerved her.

"You remember that old adage about eyes being the mirrors to the soul?" he asked. "Well, that's what yours are. The mirror to your soul. They show everything you're feeling. Everything."

Madeline looked away, embarrassed. And no doubt her eyes had told him that she found him attractive. "Then I guess I'll just take my phony smile and expressive eyes on home and let the expert take over," she said in a voice dripping with sarcasm. She started to walk away.

Chase grabbed her arm before she could take the first step. He turned her around to face him. "I'm afraid you've waited a little too late for that. Your father's headed this way with that nosy woman reporter, and they've got a photographer with them."

Madeline tried to tug her arm free. "So? You and my father can be in the pictures. It's his hotel. Not mine."

"No, it's not yours. But you wanted it. Still want it so bad you can taste it. I know all about wanting like that, Madeline." His eyes grew dark, stormy.

Surprised by Chase's reply, she stared at him, not knowing what to say. Did he feel sorry for her? Was it pity she saw in his eyes? She found that thought humiliating. She didn't need his pity or want it. "What about my phony smile? And expressive eyes? Aren't you afraid that my dislike for this merger and you will be apparent?"

"No. The pictures will probably be in black-and-white, so it won't show. But if you're worried," he said, flashing another smile at her. "You can always give one of those sweet, sultry smiles you were using on the pretty boy in the Italian suit you were with.''

She frowned, wondering who he meant.

"Blow-dried hair, toothpaste grin."

"Kyle?" Surprised by his comment, she didn't even realize that he had taken her left hand and was studying it.

"You two lovers?"

"Of course not. He's—" Furious with herself for responding, Madeline pulled her hand free. "That's none of your business."

Chase grinned. "That's where you're wrong. Everything about the hotel's my business. But we'll discuss that later. Right now you need to start smiling," he said as the cameraman and others drew near. He leaned closer and whispered in her ear, "The sweet, sultry one, Madeline. Only this time pretend it's for me."

Two

He had to give her credit, Chase decided as Madeline's lips curved up sweetly and she turned her face toward the camera. From the heated look she had leveled at him, she probably would have much preferred to slug him.

Not that he blamed her. After all, he had been the one to provoke her. He wasn't even sure why he had done it, except that the anguish in those expressive eyes of hers had caught him off guard.

And it had made him feel guilty as hell. Feeling guilty had disturbed him, even spooked him a little—almost as much as his wanting her did.

His questions about her relationship had been out of line and he knew it. For some reason, knowing she would be meeting the guy in the morning had irritated him, like a pesky mosquito bite. But her response had pleased him.

"Great," the reporter said as the photographer fired off another shot. "Now why don't we take one with Madeline in the center and, Henri, you stand over here and, Mr. McAllister, you—"

"Chase," he corrected, earning another warm look from the snoopy reporter, along with a glare from Madeline.

"...and Chase," the woman amended. "You stand right here next to Madeline. Now smile everyone."

The smile on Madeline's lips wasn't the same sultry one she had given the pretty-boy stiff with the manicured nails and three-hundred-dollar tie.

But it had the same effect. It had him wondering if her mouth was as sweet and soft and warm as it looked.

Not that he had any intention of finding out, Chase conceded as he slanted his mouth into a grin for the camera. Putting the deal together to buy into the Saint Charles had been difficult enough, especially considering his personal stake in the project. The last thing he needed was the complications a personal involvement with Madeline Charbonnet would create.

Because there would be complications. She came wrapped in an expensive package with a fancy pedigree. And while he might have learned to appreciate the finer things in life, he was strictly an off-the-rack kind of guy. As for his lineage, he would be hard-pressed to even trace his bloodlines back to his father, let alone generations of aristocrats. But even if those things didn't factor in, the fact that she was Henri Charbonnet's daughter did. That, in itself, made the notion of any relationship between them not only risky but downright foolish.

Tasting the champagne the waiter had provided, Chase waited for the photographer to stage the next shot and stole another glance at Madeline's legs. *But darned if the idea wasn't tempting.*

"Okay, everyone, lift your glasses in a toast to the new partnership," the reporter instructed.

As he raised his glass, Chase caught Madeline's eye. "To the partnership," he said, tapping his glass against hers. His grin widened at the quick spark of anger in her green eyes that preceded the camera's flash. He had no doubts that she would love to dump the contents of her glass over his head.

Chase laughed to himself. There was little chance of anything developing between them as long as she was furious with him. And dealing with Madeline Charbonnet spitting fire at him would be a lot safer.

"Thank you, Bitsy," Henri said, moving over to the reporter after the photographer finished the shots. "When do you think the story and the photos will be in the paper?"

"I'm going to try for the Friday edition."

"Excellent. And, of course, I want you to be the one who does the follow-up story on the renovations. Did I tell you they're going to be quite extensive? Every suite in the hotel is being redone," Henri said as he led the reporter away.

Chase turned back to Madeline who handed the waiter her untouched glass of champagne.

"What's the matter? House brand doesn't suit your taste buds, either?"

"What are you talking about?"

Chase took another sip from his glass. "I mean your father wanted to serve Dom Pérignon for the reception today. He wasn't at all happy at being informed that he would have to settle for the house brand."

"My father likes the best," Madeline said, tossing up her chin another notch. "There's nothing wrong with that."

"No. Not if you can afford it." He waited for her to fill the silence. When she didn't, he asked, "What about you, Madeline? You have your father's expensive tastes, too?"

He wasn't being fair, goading her like this and he knew it. But then, he hadn't counted on being moved by sad green eyes and a kissable mouth. The fact that he found her attractive was bad enough. He couldn't afford to feel sympathy for Madeline Charbonnet, too. He was much better off having her spitting fire at him.

Or in this case ice . . . because the look she directed at him could freeze water on a hot July day. "I prefer to think of myself as discerning. Just because something comes with a fancy label doesn't necessarily mean it's the best."

"No, it doesn't. Does it?" That cool, controlled smile of hers was like waving a red flag at a bull. He couldn't resist it or the chance to rattle her the way she had him. Stepping closer, he reached over to set his glass down on the table behind her. He grinned at Madeline's small intake of breath and the light shiver of awareness that ran through her. At least she was as conscious of him as he was of her, he thought, pleased by the discovery. Tempted to touch that satiny skin, he shoved his hands into his pockets. "And what about people and their jobs, Madeline?"

"I beg your pardon?" she asked, confusion clouding her eyes. Those eyes of hers really were a dead giveaway to what she was feeling.

"I was wondering if your convictions about fancy packaging extended to people and the jobs they perform within a company or say, a hotel."

"Mr. McAllister, I'm afraid you've lost me. Just what is it you're asking?"

He allowed his gaze to skim over her again. "I was wondering whether you believed a fancy package and job title makes one person or the job they do more important than another. For example, do you see your position as director of sales more important to the operation of this hotel than say... that busboy over there."

Madeline's spine stiffened. She curled her hands into fists at her side. "I'm not a snob, McAllister. Just because my father owns...owned the Saint Charles, doesn't mean I consider myself or my position of any more or any less value than anyone else's."

"I'm glad to hear that. Because I'll be meeting with key members of the hotel's staff to define and evaluate their positions. I've put you down for tomorrow morning at nine o'clock."

"But I have a breakfast appointment—"

"Be there, Madeline. Nine o'clock. Unless, of course, you'd prefer to seek other employment."

Without waiting for her reply, he turned and headed back into the reception room.

You're a real bastard, McAllister, Chase told himself as he shook hands with some banker. But then, being a bastard was better than allowing the classy Ms. Madeline Charbonnet to sneak past his conscience and appeal to whatever noble instincts he might have. He wanted her, and wanting her was a weakness. And one of the first lessons he had learned living at St. Mark's and the succession of foster homes that followed was people used your weaknesses against you if you let them.

Given half a chance, he had no doubt that Madeline Charbonnet with her silken skin and made-for-kissing mouth would slip right past his safeguards and cut his heart out if he gave her half a chance.

He had no intention of giving her that chance. Having Madeline hate him was not only safer, but would also make it a hell of a lot easier for him when he brought Henri Charbonnet down.

The jerk. The big arrogant jerk. Madeline was fuming as she glanced at her watch for a third time in as many minutes. He had forced her to cancel her breakfast meeting with Kyle, only to have his secretary call her at eight forty-five and postpone their meeting until two o'clock—which had forced her to reschedule her afternoon appointments, as well.

And now the louse had kept her waiting for over twenty minutes. It was probably another stupid ploy to keep her off balance. But this time she had no intention of letting him succeed.

Madeline tapped her nails impatiently on the thick folder resting on her lap. She could hardly wait to shove the sales forecast reports under his nose. Obviously when he'd left instructions for her to bring them to the meeting, he hadn't expected her to be able to produce them so quickly.

Irritated, Madeline stood and paced the length of the office he had claimed for himself. The desk was piled high with a mountain of reports, computer printouts and financial statements. The man had certainly been busy in the last forty-eight hours. From what she had gleaned from the staff, he had spent little time in the suite of rooms he had confiscated as his living quarters. Evidently, when he wasn't in his office, he was busy sticking his nose into all corners of the hotel's operations.

One thing was certain. Chase McAllister had certainly made his presence felt at the hotel—at least among the female staff. If one more secretary or housekeeper used the word *hunk* in conjunction with his name, she would scream.

Slapping the folder against her leg, Madeline retraced her path across the room. Maybe she should have just stuck to her original game plan and resigned. In a city booming with convention business, it wouldn't have taken her too long to find another job. Another job certainly would have been healthier than standing here contemplating ways to murder Chase McAllister.

If only she hadn't allowed her father to extract a promise from her last night to stay on temporarily for the sake of appearances. *Oh, face it, Madeline. The promise you gave your father isn't the reason you stayed.* She had stayed on out of sheer stubbornness and she knew it. Because resigning was just what Chase McAllister expected and probably wanted her to do. It was the only thing that explained the little scene he had engineered between them yesterday at the reception.

Well, she refused to give him the satisfaction. If he wanted her out of here, he was going to have to fire her. And she wasn't going to make it easy for him to do it, either. She was very good at what she did, and she had the sales bookings to prove it. If the dirty rat thought her sales production would provide him with the necessary grounds for her termination, he had just better think again.

Madeline whirled around at the sound of the door opening and watched the rodent himself walk in holding a plastic foam container with two cups on top. Her heart did a quick tap dance that she steadfastly ignored. Instead, she decided to give the chauvinist a dose of his own medicine.

It's payback time, McAllister, she thought silently, and made a point of looking him over the same way he had done her the previous day. Taking her time, she noted the scuff marks on his shoes, the smudges of something that resembled grease on the gray slacks that matched the jacket she had seen hooked behind the door. Enjoying herself, Madeline flicked her gaze over his white dress shirt rolled up to the elbows, to the opened collar which had lost its crispness as well as the tie that any self-respecting hotelier would have had neatly knotted around it.

She made a deliberately slow sweep over his chin and stamped down the questions and flicker of empathy the scar aroused. She continued her blatant perusal, resting momentarily on that wicked mouth of his that seemed to want to kick into a grin, before lifting her gaze to meet his.

The blue eyes that looked back at her were gleaming with amusement that matched the smile spreading across his lips.

Madeline gritted her teeth. *The man was insufferable,* she thought, irked that he had found her once-over tactics amusing, while she had found his so unnerving. "You're late," she told him, deliberately looking at her watch.

"Yeah, I know. Sorry about that. There was a problem with one of the water heaters, and I went to give maintenance a hand." He kicked the door shut and walked over to the desk.

"I didn't realize you were a plumber," she said coolly.

He shrugged, the ice in her voice having no effect on him. "Not all of us are born into the hotel business, Princess. Some of us have to work our way up. It's not a bad way to learn all the ins and outs of making the business work." He set the container down and removed the two cups from atop it. "My first hotel job was as a busboy at fifteen. I moved up to waiter the following year. Have a seat." He gestured to the chair across from his desk.

Wary, Madeline picked her way across the carpet and sat down in the chair he had indicated. She crossed her legs and caught the quirk of his lips as his eyes followed the movement. Madeline tugged on the hem of her skirt and wished the thing were several inches longer. "Mr. McAllister—"

"What about you?" he asked, taking his seat. "What was your first hotel job?"

"Front desk clerk," she answered without thinking.

"Lucky you. I didn't get to work the front desk until I was in college."

Well, that certainly put her in her place. But not for the life of her would she admit to him that she would have preferred to wait on tables as he had, but her father had refused to allow her to do so. "I've got a news flash for you McAllister, I may not have bussed tables, but I've worked at least a dozen other lesser positions in this hotel, from catering assistant to file clerk, and not one of those positions was ever handed to me because my father owned the hotel. I've worked darn hard to become director of sales, and I was appointed to that position because I'm good at what I do— not because of who my father is."

"No need to get all prickly, Princess. I was making a statement, not an accusation."

"You certainly could have fooled me, Mr. McAllister."

Chase smiled. "You know, you're the only person I know who can manage to say my name so prettily and still make it sound like an insult. Since we're going to be working together, why don't we dispense with the formalities? You call me Chase and I'll call you..."

She glared at him, daring him to call her *Princess* again.

"...and I'll call you Madeline."

Refusing to respond to his sexy little grin, Madeline leaned forward slightly. "Are we going to be working together, *Chase?* I wasn't at all sure we would be. In fact, I had the distinct impression you were hoping I would quit."

"Can't imagine why you'd think that."

"It probably had something to do with your none-too-subtle comments yesterday about needing 'capable' people in the sales department."

"You didn't think I was subtle? I thought I was being subtle."

"Let me put it to you this way. I've come across steam-rollers that were more subtle than you."

He paused, seeming to give it some thought, then shrugged. "Subtlety never was one of my virtues. But that's okay, I've got lots of others."

"Obviously humility isn't one of them."

Chase laughed. "Afraid that's one of the virtues the good brothers at St. Mark's didn't succeed in teaching me. For some reason, I equated being humble with being subservient, and I never much liked taking orders."

"How interesting," Madeline returned. "Neither do I."

"Know what I think?"

"I don't have any idea what you think, Chase. And to be quite honest, I'm not the least bit interested."

He smiled again, and Madeline was hard-pressed not to respond to that engaging curve of his lips. "I think you're just too sensitive. Otherwise, why would you jump to the conclusion that my comments were directed toward you?" he asked, popping open the plastic foam container.

The scent of warm blueberry muffins wafted across the desk. Madeline's mouth watered, reminding her that she had worked through lunch to complete the sales forecasts he had requested and she still hadn't eaten. She tugged her attention back to him. "Just a guess. Or maybe it has something to do with the fact that you've been demanding reports from my department nonstop since you got here."

"Like I said, you're too sensitive. I've been requesting reports from all the departments, not just yours. Want one?" he asked, nudging the box of muffins toward her.

Madeline thought of the skirt to her green suit, remembering how snug it had felt going on that morning. Just smelling those sugar-laden muffins would probably add an inch to her hips. "No thanks," she finally managed to say. She held out the file she had brought. "Here are the last six months' sales figures for my department and a forecast for the next six."

Chase took the folder and set it aside and went back to the muffins. "These things are addictive," he said, peeling back the paper wrapping. He sank his teeth into the muffin and the expression that crossed his face was one of pure ecstasy.

Madeline shifted uncomfortably in her seat. No wonder the women in the hotel were fussing over him, the man made something as simple as eating a muffin look like a sensual feast. "If you'd like to go over the projections—"

"In a minute. How about some coffee? I brought an extra cup up from the restaurant." He pushed the offering toward her. "Go ahead, I had them put sugar and cream in both of them."

Madeline pulled off the plastic top and took a sip. "I thought most Yankees drank their coffee black."

"I suspect most of them do. But then, I'm not a Yankee. I'm a Southerner, just like you." He started in on another muffin.

Madeline arched her brow. "I understood you were from New Jersey."

"I live in New Jersey now," he said, reaching for another muffin. "But I was born in Mississippi. Sure you don't want one of these?"

"Maybe just half."

Chase divided the muffin in two and slid the paper napkin with her portion over to her. He popped the other piece into his mouth.

"I would never have guessed. About your being from the South. You don't have any trace of a Mississippi accent." Madeline broke off a small bite.

"That's because I didn't live there long enough to get one. My mother moved us to New Orleans after my father died. I was still in diapers at the time."

Intrigued, Madeline asked, "Does your mother still live here?"

Something sad and haunting flickered in his eyes a moment, making Madeline regret she had asked the question. "She died when I was eight."

"I'm sorry." The words seemed so inadequate.

Chase shrugged and finished off his coffee. "It was a long time ago."

But it was obvious he still felt the loss. She had been twice his age when her own mother had passed away, and she still missed her. So did her father. "I'm sure if your mother were here, she would be very proud to see what you've made of your life."

"You might say it's because of her that I'm here now. She loved old hotels . . . particularly this one."

"And she shared that love with you," Madeline concluded. There was something oddly sweet and romantic about the notion, and she found herself softening towards Chase. "That's what happened to me, too. My grandfather adored this hotel. I used to spend hours listening to him tell stories about it and the people who had stayed here. I fell in love with the place and couldn't wait until I grew up so that I could work here, too." Madeline warmed at the memory. Pressing the last crumbs of the muffin on the napkin with her fingertip, she licked them off. "I've never wanted to do anything else but be a hotelier."

Glancing up, Madeline found Chase watching her. There was something hot and hungry in the way he stared at her mouth. Her pulse scattered and for the space of a heartbeat she wondered what it would be like to kiss him.

Disturbed by her thoughts, even more disturbed that he might know what she had been thinking, Madeline jerked to her feet. "I better go. I have a meeting with the travel coordinator for an accounting firm about booking the company's continuing-education seminar at the hotel." She started for the door, anxious to leave before she made a complete fool of herself. "Let me know if you have any questions about the reports.

"Madeline, wait."

She stopped at the door; her heart raced like a Thoroughbred as he moved closer. "This is an important account. It means one hundred room nights, plus fifty table covers. I don't want to be late."

"I'm glad you're so conscientious." His lips curved into another of those sexy-as-sin grins of his. "But I'm sure you wouldn't want to meet your client with that smudge of blueberry on your chin."

"Blue—"

He caught her hand when she would have wiped at her face, and ran his thumb along her jaw, to the edge of her mouth, across her bottom lip.

A breath shuddered through Madeline at the sensual impact of his touch. Her skin heated, tingled. Like a doe trapped in the lights of an oncoming car, she was unable to move a muscle as he lowered his head.

His lips were hot, coaxing and utterly intoxicating. Chase lifted his head a fraction and Madeline heard a moan between them. She prayed it hadn't come from her, was afraid that it had.

And then she forgot about praying, forgot about thinking, as Chase lowered his head and covered her mouth once more.

Three

"**I** was wrong. Your skin's even softer than I imagined. Like silk," Chase said, tracing a line with his finger from her jaw to the corner of her mouth. His hand shook at the force of feelings rumbling inside of him. Not once in his thirty-four years had a simple kiss rocked him so soundly. "A man could go crazy wondering if the rest of you is as soft as your mouth." He smiled as a shudder went through her, and dipped his head for another taste.

Madeline pushed lightly against his shoulders. Her fingers curled into his shirt. "Chase."

His name was a muffled whisper from her lips... her incredibly soft, moist lips that were as addictive as the hotel's blueberry muffins. And infinitely sweeter.

Damn, if he didn't hear bells ringing. It was either that or a warning signal from his body, letting him know that it would never be satisfied with just a single kiss.

"Chase," she repeated. This time her hands were pressing against his chest, putting some space between them. "The telephone... it's ringing."

As though to mock him, the phone jangled once more, then stopped, leaving only the sound of their own ragged breathing and the ticking of the clock to fill the silence. Opening his eyes, he felt reality come back to him in a rush.

Chase swore silently and took a step back. *What in the hell was I thinking of to kiss her like that?* Hadn't he already decided against it? Being attracted to Madeline Charbonnet was the last thing he wanted or needed in his life. "I'm sorry. I didn't mean for that to happen. It was a mistake."

"A mistake?"

"Yes." Irritated, confused, he wasn't sure who he was angrier with—himself for kissing her or her for making him want to do it again. He shoved his hands in his pockets to keep from reaching for her a second time. "It was inappropriate of me to kiss you."

"Inappropriate?" She repeated the word as though she had bitten into a lemon and found the taste sour.

Chase cut a glance at her and noted the stubborn angle of her chin, her hands clenched into tight fists at her sides. Her outraged expression only added to his agitation. "You don't have to go all prissy and proper on me, Princess. I'm sure I'm not the first man who's kissed you. Hell, unless he's a saint or a priest, any man from eight to eighty would be hard-pressed not to contemplate kissing you at least once."

Her eyes smoldered. "And you're neither," she said between clenched teeth.

"No. I'm not." He shoved his hand through his hair. "Look, I said I was sorry. Kissing you was a mistake. It won't happen again."

"You're right. It was a mistake and it had better not happen again," she replied, squaring her shoulders. Her breasts thrust against the jacket of her suit, burning him with thoughts of feeling them pressed against him.

A burst of desire rocketed through him with the heat and speed of a shooting star. Cursing himself again for his reaction to her, Chase looked away, still not understanding or liking the fact that she affected him as she did.

"There are laws against mauling female employees, Mr. McAllister," Madeline continued in that sweet, prim voice of hers. "I hope you don't make it a practice."

Chase whipped around at the accusation. "The 'mauling' wasn't exactly one-sided, *Ms.* Charbonnet."

"*You* kissed me."

"And *you* kissed me back," he countered, daring her to deny it and feeling a measure of satisfaction when she didn't. "But just for the record the answer's no. I don't make a practice of becoming involved with people who work for me."

The comment brought her head snapping up again. Her eyes flashed with cold fury. "I don't work for you."

"You work for the hotel. And like it or not, I'm in charge of the hotel." Chase was irritated with himself and with her for pretending she hadn't been equally affected by the kiss. He itched to kiss her again and wipe that snooty look off her face. But that would be another mistake, one he would be wise to avoid.

That dainty little chin of hers rose another notch. "Funny, I thought you were merely an employee of Majestic Hotels—not the owner. In fact, I wasn't even sure you had a title other than troubleshooter."

"Oh, I've got a whole string of titles, but troubleshooter fits well enough. Probably better than most of the others since I tend to enjoy trouble. You might even say I thrive on it."

She arched one dark brow. "Eliminating it or causing it?"

"I'm very good at both."

"I'll just bet you are," she said, her voice as cool as her green eyes.

It was the coolness that got to him. And he decided to push her a tad harder—partly because he wanted to watch those expressive eyes of hers shift from cold to hot, partly because he wanted to make sure that things between them wouldn't go any further. Right now, that thought didn't appeal to him—not when just looking at her set his hormones back two decades and had him feeling like a raw

teenager again. So he pushed the buttons he was pretty sure
would make her do the shoving. "And while it's against my
own personal policy to become involved with an employee,
if you're planning to resign anyway, I guess there's no reason the two of us couldn't engage in some good old-
fashioned mutual lust."

Chase caught her hand before it made contact with his
cheek. She tugged, but he held on to her wrist.

Fury shimmered in her eyes. "Don't hold your breath,
McAllister. Despite what you'd like, I have no intention of
resigning. And as for their being any mutual lust, not in this
lifetime, buster."

"No?" He stroked his thumb across her wrist.

Madeline averted her gaze to some point past his shoulder. "While I'll admit to some elemental curiosity on my
part—"

"Curiosity?" He moved a fraction closer and smiled as
her pulse skittered beneath his thumb.

"All right, attraction," she said, glaring at him. "For
some perverse reason, I do find you attractive in the most
basic animalistic sort of way. That's why I allowed you to
kiss me."

"You allowed me to kiss you," he repeated in that same
prim voice she had used.

"Yes."

Chase chuckled. "Princess, I've got a news bulletin for
you. Whether you like it or not, that kiss wasn't one-sided."
He leaned even closer and saw the awareness register in her
eyes. He didn't bother to hide his grin of satisfaction,
pleased that she was as affected by him as he was by her.
"And as much as we both might like to repeat the experience, I'm afraid we're not going to. You see, I meant what
I said, I don't believe in becoming involved with employees—even when the employee happens to be a sweet little
Southern belle like yourself. But if you think resisting me is
going to be a problem for you, I'll certainly understand if
you want to reconsider your decision to stay on at the hotel."

"Oh, I think I can resist you, *Mr.* McAllister." She yanked her wrist free.

"Think so?"

"I know so," she informed him.

"You know, Princess, that almost sounds like a dare. Makes me tempted to prove you wrong. I can be quite charming when I set my mind to it." He flashed her another grin.

Her back went stiff as a board. "Then I suggest you save your so-called charm and killer smiles for another victim. Because I'm not interested."

"No?" he asked, moving his mouth within a whisper of hers.

"No," she said firmly, meeting his gaze. "You see, I've never been particularly fond of pork. And you really are a first-rate pig, McAllister. As for my resigning, don't hold your breath." The smile she gave him was as hard as day-old French bread. "Now unless you want to discover what it feels like to be kneed in the groin by this sweet Southern belle, I suggest you back off."

Chase stepped back instantly, never doubting for a second that she would make good on her threat if he didn't.

Madeline turned and jerked the door open.

"Oh, and, Princess," Chase said, staying her movement.

"What?" she snapped impatiently.

"Don't forget about the staff meeting tomorrow morning. I'd hate to see you miss another one."

Madeline slipped in the rear door of the conference room and eased into an empty seat in the back row, just as her father began to speak.

Punctual by nature, she felt foolish arriving late deliberately. No doubt doing so was a perverse reaction to Chase's parting remark the previous afternoon. At least she had overcome her initial inclination not to come at all. That was probably what he had hoped she would do—give him a reason to dismiss her.

Well, she had no intention of falling in with his plans. Now more than ever she was determined to stay on at the hotel, if for no other reason than to prove to her father and to Chase that they were both wrong about her. Not only was she capable of running the hotel, but she also was capable of resisting Chase McAllister.

"I called this meeting today to thank each of you for your service and dedication to the Saint Charles Hotel. Many of you have been with the hotel and with the Charbonnet family for a great number of years..."

Madeline tried to concentrate on her father's remarks, but unerringly her gaze wandered from her father to Chase.

He stood with his feet slightly apart, his hands clasped in front of him. Yesterday's wrinkled shirt and soiled slacks had been exchanged for a dark olive suit that made his eyes appear more green than blue. The wheat-colored hair, although still too long to conform to what she considered acceptable in a hotel like the Saint Charles, had been neatly combed and tamed into place.

Madeline looked at his hands, remembering the warmth and gentleness of those fingers as he had caressed her face. But his touch had not prepared her for the feel of his mouth hot and hungry against her own.

Heat rushed to her cheeks at the memory of how completely she had given herself to him in that kiss. *How could I have kissed him like that? With such abandon? With such wanton need?*

And the rat...he had known just how affected she had been by that kiss. She had seen it in his expression, had tasted it on his lips. Despite her protests, she had been stunned down to her toes and lost in the dizzying pleasure of Chase McAllister's kiss.

She had made a complete and utter fool of herself. And to make matters worse, the idiot had actually apologized for kissing her—which had only made her feel even more foolish, more embarrassed and angrier still.

The man had an ego the size of the Mississippi River and her quick-fire response had fed it beautifully. What she wouldn't give to be able to take him down a peg or two. Irritation simmering anew inside her, Madeline glanced up and studied his sinfully tanned face, his clever and tempting mouth. Her one and only consolation had been the nagging suspicion that he had been just as much caught off guard, just as shaken as she had been by the kiss.

"And even though Majestic Hotels is now one of the owners of the Saint Charles, I want to assure you that nothing is going to change..."

Madeline watched in fascination as that amused, confident glint in his eyes dimmed, then slipped into a frown that spread to his wicked mouth. A shiver of uneasiness shimmied down her spine as his expression hardened. She shifted her attention to the object of his gaze—her father.

"This hotel has always been run by a Charbonnet," her father continued, his voice booming. "It was run by my father and his father before him and I will continue..."

Frustration came over Madeline in waves as her father went into his spiel about the unbroken line of Charbonnet males who had run the hotel. No matter how many times she heard the familiar tale, she still smarted at the injustice of not being allowed the same opportunity.

But she had formulated some plans of her own during the long, sleepless night. While she could do nothing to negate Majestic's ownership interest in the Saint Charles, she could make it work to her advantage. The hotel desperately needed an assistant general manager, and who better for the job than someone who knew and loved the property so intimately. Somehow, someway, she would convince the new owners and her father to give her that chance.

And if that meant working with the insufferable Chase McAllister for the short time he would be here, then so be it. He wasn't the first man she had encountered with more than his fair share of sex appeal. But, Lord, he was the first one whose kisses had proved lethal to her.

As though he sensed her scrutiny, Chase turned and looked directly at her. Madeline swallowed, struck at first by the coldness in those blue eyes, then by the burst of heat and hunger as his gaze moved boldly over her face and mouth.

A breath stuck in her throat. Her lungs refused to work. But not for the life of her would she feed his ego further by being the first to look away.

"I will continue in my capacity as the hotel's executive director and..."

Chase slid his gaze back to her father, and Madeline was able to breathe again. As her heart rate returned to normal, she continued to study him. Judging from his expression, her father's comments were not appreciated. Madeline rubbed her hands along her arms, unable to shake the feeling that her father had underestimated the man.

"Thank you, Henri," Chase said, coming up beside her father and taking command of the podium. "I would like to join Henri and add Majestic Hotels' thanks for your service and dedication to the Saint Charles. I also would like to tell you about some of the changes that you can expect..."

Ten minutes later after advising the staff of his firm's investment in the hotel and in the employees, he ran through some of the changes that would be taking place not only in the hotel's appearance but its method of operation as well. "And while there are no plans to cut back on staff, every expenditure, every salary has to be justified," he said, looking directly at Madeline. "And anyone not pulling his or her weight, will be replaced."

Refusing to be intimidated, Madeline held his gaze and pulled one of his own tricks. She smiled at him.

"Our mutual goal—"

Chase's hesitation and the shifting of his gaze was soothing balm to her ego.

"Our mutual goal," he began again, "is to restore the hotel to the first-class reputation and prosperity it once enjoyed. And with that restoration we hope that instead of layoffs we will be hiring additional employees."

A round of applause followed and then he opened the floor for questions. A hand went up from one of the new members of the sales staff. "Mr. McAllister, will you be overseeing just the accounting or will you be involved in the sales department, too?"

Chase directed one of his killer-watt smiles toward the female, and Madeline knew without looking that the other woman was just short of falling at the man's feet. She shifted in her seat, irritated by his easy charm.

"I'll be involved in *all* aspects of the hotel's operation. The sales department has been doing a good job, but I think it can do better. I have several ideas in that direction, and I plan to work closely with Madeline Charbonnet in the implementation of those ideas. I will also be working with Henri Charbonnet on the operation of the hotel."

A good job? Madeline gritted her teeth at his response. While no hotel operated at one-hundred-percent capacity, she and her department had worked small miracles keeping the hotel rooms filled, with occupancy rates often exceeding eighty percent. Did he have any idea what a difficult property this was to sell, particularly when she was competing with the big chains for convention and tourism business? She certainly didn't need him to tell her how to do her job. Madeline stood up, not waiting for him to call upon her. "Mr. McAllister, just how long do you plan to be at the Saint Charles?" The sooner he went back to his East Coast offices the better.

If he heard the challenge in her voice, he ignored it. His eyes twinkled with laughter. "As long as it takes to see the hotel through the renovations and get the operations on track."

"And can we assume that once the new systems are in place and the renovations have begun that you'll be returning home?"

"As I think I mentioned to you yesterday, Ms. Charbonnet, New Orleans is home for me."

Madeline's heartbeat quickened. She licked her lips, trying not to panic. She didn't want to think about that conversation yesterday or the sadness that had come into his eyes when he'd spoken of his mother. She especially didn't want to remember the heated kisses that had followed. "But it was my understanding you wouldn't be involved in the hotel's operations on a day-to-day basis. I understood that once the new systems were implemented and the renovations underway you would be returning to your firm's headquarters. I was told you would only need to return here on a monthly basis to check the hotel's progress."

"That was the original idea. But there's been a change of plans," Chase said, delighting in the wariness that crept into her eyes. Damn, if that mouth of hers didn't look even more kissable this morning. Dressed in her prim, checkered suit and silky white blouse, there was something sexy as hell about those pouty lips painted fire engine red.

And incredibly arousing, Chase decided, as she flicked her tongue in and out to moisten her lips. "I'll be staying on until the renovations are completed and the hotel's grand opening celebration is held in the fall," he explained.

"But that's at least six months away," Madeline replied.

"Yes, it is." And an interesting six months it was going to be, Chase decided, as he continued to field questions. When Jamison, Majestic's chairman, had suggested that he stay on-site for the duration of the hotel's renovations, he had been opposed. But after a few days' observance of Henri Charbonnet's spending habits, he had to admit that it would take more than monthly financial meetings and reports to keep the hotel within budget. Since he had been the one to bring the Saint Charles deal to the table, and had a vested interest of his own in the project, it only made sense that he be the one to stay on and oversee it.

Being the one to shorten Henri Charbonnet's leash would be a headache and a pleasure, but it was one he had looked forward to for a long time.

And the daughter? His gaze drifted back to Madeline and he found himself contemplating another taste of her lips. She was the source of another kind of ache altogether.

That's the price you pay for eight months of self-imposed celibacy, McAllister. But even as he thought it, he knew it wasn't entirely true. Despite the line he had fed Madeline yesterday, he had never been a man to engage in meaningless sex for sex's sake. And while it had been some time since his last relationship had ended, abstinence didn't even begin to explain his response to her.

No. Madeline Charbonnet would have been a difficult specimen to resist under the best of circumstances. It was just his rotten luck that the first female he felt tempted by in ages would turn out to be Henri Charbonnet's daughter.

Trouble. That's what a relationship with Madeline Charbonnet would mean. And if she stayed on at the hotel as he suspected she would, it was just a matter of time before the two of them landed in bed. It was inevitable. He had come to that conclusion during the night. And to fight the inevitable would be pointless. So, the two of them might as well enjoy it.

Chase smiled and turned his gaze back to the green-eyed siren sitting stiff and straight in her chair. She arched her brow in that duchess-to-peasant manner.

It was all the challenge he needed. Chase winked at her, then shifted his attention to the staff. "Now, ladies and gentlemen, if there are no other questions, I suggest we all get back to work. We have a hotel to run."

And he had an old score to settle and a sweet, tempting piece of trouble that he was looking forward to coaxing into his bed.

Four

"Come in," Chase called out in response to the knock at his office door.

"Ellen wasn't at her desk," Madeline explained, hesitating in the doorway.

He glanced up from the computer screen. "I know. She wasn't feeling well, so I sent her home. Come on in." The figures he had been reviewing became a forgotten jumble as he took in the sight of her.

Today's outfit was yet another suit, Chase noted and he wondered idly just how many of the things she owned. Navy with round gold buttons and braid trim, this particular number reminded him of a military uniform. Albeit, he had never seen a uniform filled out quite so nicely, he mused, a smile of appreciation twitching at his lips. Nor had he seen any uniform that had been cut to dip at the waist and skim several inches above the knees to reveal a tantalizing glimpse of thigh.

She walked across the almond-colored carpet, and Chase couldn't help but notice the gentle sway of her hips as she moved.

"I had a message on my desk that you wanted to see me," she said stiffly.

"That's right," Chase replied, reluctantly shifting his attention from her legs to her face. Judging from the rigid line of her stance and the coolness in her expression, she had noted his scrutiny and hadn't appreciated it. He definitely intended to work on changing her mind on that score. But for now, it was back to business. "I wanted to go over the budget and projections you submitted for your department. Just give me a minute to finish this report and then we'll get started. Have a seat." He motioned to the chair across from his desk, then went back to punching numbers into the terminal.

Chase stared at the computer screen, but he was keenly aware of Madeline seated across from him. Forcing himself to concentrate, he plugged in more figures and watched them pop up on the screen. She shifted in her seat. Unable to resist, Chase slanted another glance her way. She had crossed her legs, and the toe of one navy pump tapped at the empty air impatiently. Chase slid his gaze up the long hose-covered leg and smiled. The one good thing about her suits, he thought as he admired the view, the skirts always offered him a glimpse of her legs.

Suddenly Madeline's foot stilled. She uncrossed her legs and stood. "Listen, I have some sales calls to return, and since you're obviously busy, too, maybe it would be better if you just sent me a memo with your comments about the report and I'll get back to you."

Chase sighed. Sitting back in his chair, he steepled his fingers and looked up at Madeline. The woman reminded him of a skittish colt. By all means a Thoroughbred—with her mane of dark hair and jewel-colored eyes—but skittish all the same. He looked at those pouty lips. Desire stirred, then twisted in his gut as he remembered that combination of sweetness and heat when he had kissed her. He slanted his gaze to her eyes and caught the flicker of awareness.

So she remembered the kiss, too.

And it made her nervous.

He made her nervous, Chase amended as he watched the wariness creep into her expressive eyes.

Good, he thought, pleased by the realization. At least he hadn't been the only one whose thoughts had been disrupted by the memory of that kiss. He had found himself eager to repeat the experience just to see if it had been as explosive as he remembered. His conscience, coupled with the demands on his time, had prevented him from following through. Guilt over the prospect of seducing her while he set out to destroy her father had made him question his decision to do so. The implementation of the new systems, entertaining proposals on the renovations and two trips back to New Jersey had settled the matter for him. At least, he had thought so.

Until now.

Up until now he had managed barely more than a few words with her during the past few weeks. And except for an occasional glimpse of her about the hotel, he had seen far less of Madeline Charbonnet than he had expected. What surprised him was how frequently she had inserted herself into his thoughts—a rarity for him, considering the fact that women usually garnered his attention only for the period of time they spent in his company.

Not so with Madeline. Even when she wasn't around or taking up space in his thoughts, she made her presence felt. From what he had observed, Madeline was the Charbonnet the employees turned to when a problem arose—not her father. Madeline was the one everyone went to for answers. Charbonnet had been foolish not to let his daughter take over the hotel. If he had, she might have been able to save him. Lucky for him the old man hadn't.

"I'll just check my In box this afternoon and get back to you as soon as—"

"Oh, I think we can dispense with the memos and save a few trees," Chase offered. He watched her hand clench, then unclench to smooth the line of her skirt. Yes, he definitely made Madeline Charbonnet nervous. Now that he thought about it, he wondered if their lack of contact had been by design. Had she been avoiding him? Conveniently slipping out of her department or the hotel on sales calls whenever he was around? If so, her running days were over. "Besides, I much prefer dealing with you in person than on paper."

She narrowed her eyes. "What about your report?" She inclined her head to the computer screen.

"Done." To emphasize his point, he hit the Command button, and the printer across the room began spitting out pages. "Have a seat."

When Madeline did so without arguing, Chase couldn't resist teasing, "What, no argument?"

Her green eyes flashed. "Would it do any good?"

"No," he agreed and offered her another smile. "I guess we're getting to know each other after all."

"You said you wanted to discuss my department's budget," Madeline said, her expression as chilly as her tone.

"I do." Chase retrieved the folder that held the report she had prepared, outlining her department's projected sales and expenditures for the next twelve months. He removed it from the file and placed it on his desk.

"Is there a problem?" she asked, a hint of concern lacing her voice. Chase noted that her eyes had darted to the report and zeroed in on the items circled in red.

"Just a few questions."

"If you're worried I've overestimated the sales projections to make myself look good, I assure you I haven't. I didn't just pull those figures out of the sky. Those numbers are based on past business and a nominal share of what I believe we can realistically anticipate getting from the convention market." Moving to the edge of her seat, she continued, "I went through the Tourist Commission's list of conventions for the next twelve months, the number of visitors they anticipate coming to the city and the number of rooms that will be needed. While you may think my figures seem a bit optimistic, I'm confident we can hit those numbers."

"So am I. In fact, I'd be surprised if you didn't surpass them."

That seemed to take the starch out of her sails. She leaned back in her seat, but remained silent.

"The truth is, I thought your projections were more cautious than optimistic. But that's not what I wanted to discuss with you." He flipped through the report and found the real items that had snagged his attention and made him send for her. "I was more interested in some of the expenditures you've projected for the department. There seemed to be quite a number of items coded to sales marketing that don't directly involve any advertising."

"Not all of the hotel's marketing is done in newspaper and magazine ads."

"I'm aware of that. But you have quite a number of entertainment expenses, membership dues and charitable donations in your marketing budget. I wondered how relative they were to selling rooms at the hotel."

Something wicked gleamed in her eyes. The trace of a smile played about her lips. "You'd be surprised just how relative those entertainment expenditures and donations are to the hotel's business. Obviously you aren't familiar with the way business is done here."

"Why don't you enlighten me."

"All right, I will," she told him, seeming to grow more confident with each second that passed. "It's quite simple, really. This is an upscale hotel that caters to a distinguished clientele—clientele who belong to select organizations."

"You mean rich people."

"I mean individuals with discerning tastes who want more services and amenities than the average chain hotel can offer them and are willing to pay for it," she informed him.

"Go on."

"A large portion of that clientele happen to be locals. They belong to prominent organizations and prefer to do business with fellow members when they can. Most of them also have some pet cause or another that they support. In exchange for donations to their various causes, the hotel receives their patronage in the form of bookings from their businesses and their out-of-town clients."

"In other words you need to be one of the gang."

"For the most part," Madeline agreed.

"And you don't think the hotel would get that patronage without those memberships and donations?" Chase asked, not bothering to hide his cynicism.

"I know we wouldn't." She met his gaze evenly, confidently. "You may think you know everything there is to know about the hotel business, McAllister, but you've never done business in this city before. That old adage 'It's not what you know, but who you know' could have been penned with New Orleans in mind. The people here are close-knit. They might welcome your tourist dollars, but they won't offer you or any outsider an easy entrée into the community."

Chase laughed at the dig. "Oh, I'm very much aware of how the locals, particularly those in the mainstream of society, close ranks to outsiders like me. But you forget, Madeline, I have you and your father—members of that close-knit little social circle—to smooth the way for me."

Madeline sat silent and stone-faced across from him, and he couldn't resist the urge to shake that composure of hers. "And any smoothing that you can't do, the money Majestic will be pumping into the local economy for the renovation project should do the trick." He leaned forward in his chair. "But make no mistake. I intend not only to retain this hotel's current client base, but to expand it. I also intend to capture a much larger share of the convention trade. In fact, doing so will be part of the director of sales job. Your job. So, if you're not up to the task, you'd better let me know now."

The smile she gave him was laced with saccharine. "Like I told you before, McAllister, I'm not going anywhere—not without a fight. And as for earning my salary, don't worry, I will."

"I intend to see that you do."

"I never doubted for a second that you would," she returned evenly. "Now did you really have some questions or did you call me here just to deliver your little threat?"

"I never make threats, Princess. Only promises."

She shrugged.

The gesture was cool, disdainful and made him want to grab that stubborn jaw of hers, cover her pouty mouth with his own and watch the prim princess turn to fire in his arms. Instead, he picked up the report. "But in answer to your question, yes. I do have some questions."

"Like what?"

"Like this twenty-five hundred dollars allocated to the sales department for the REX dinner party. If my memory serves me correctly, REX is the carnival organization your father belongs to, isn't it?"

"Yes, it is." She tossed up her chin. "What of it?"

Her cool little reply irritated him more than it should have. Or maybe it was the thought of Henri Charbonnet using the hotel and its assets for his own purposes the same way he used people. The same way he had once used Katie McAllister. Chase leaned forward. "So how do you justify charging off a twenty-five-hundred-dollar dinner party for your father's carnival club cronies as a promotional expense?" he asked, pleased at the deceptive softness of his tone, given the strong feelings racing through him. It was this kind of abuse that he was looking forward to bringing to an end. He didn't want to see Madeline get caught in the cross fire. But if she did, then so be it.

"I justify it by telling you that the men who attend that party are among the wealthiest and most influential in the city. They have the ability to send tens of thousands of dollars to this hotel in room nights and catering functions."

"And how many room nights and catering functions do they send to the hotel? How much return does the hotel get in exchange for wining and dining your father's cronies?"

Madeline hesitated. "I don't know exactly. I would need to check the sales figures and catering reports from last year's bookings and—"

"Don't bother." He already knew the return was minimal. And it galled him to hear Madeline scramble to cover for her father. What disturbed him even more was the fact that he found her loyalty so appealing. "I've already deleted it from your department's budget."

"You can't do that," she said, coming to her feet.

"I already have. As an owner, your father can allocate a limited amount of money for marketing. I've moved the dinner party to that account, and the cost for it will come out of his budget—not the sales department's."

"Fine," she said, her voice flat. "Were there any other questions you had about *my* department's budget? Or perhaps I should ask if there are any other decisions you've already made that you'd like to share with me."

Chase tossed down the report and sat back, taking in the stubborn tilt of her chin, the defiance flashing in those green eyes. He couldn't help wondering what those eyes would look like simmering with passion instead of anger. He intended to find out. "Princess, there are quite a number of things I'd like to share with you," he said smiling. "And the department's budget isn't one of them."

She looked so regal staring down her pretty nose at him, and damn if he didn't find even her haughtiness a turn on. Chase shifted in his seat, regretting that he didn't have the time to pursue those other things with her now. He fully intended to do so later. "But right now, I have a few more questions about the budget."

Thirty minutes later Chase sat back in his chair, more than a little impressed with Madeline Charbonnet, and unaccountably annoyed by her at the same time. Except for the dinner party for her father and his cronies, every expenditure had been carefully researched and chosen to produce maximum benefit and exposure for the hotel. Each item would bring a healthy return on the dollar. She had answered each of his questions politely and professionally, showing none of the heat of their initial exchange.

Damn it. He preferred the hot-tempered brunette with fire in her eyes to this cool-as-ice businesswoman seated across from him.

"As you've so kindly pointed out to me, the hotel is a business. So unless you have any more items that need an explanation, I'll get back to work now. I certainly want to be sure that I earn my salary." Madeline stood.

"Just a minute."

She paused.

"What about this donation you listed here for the Historic Preservation Society."

Madeline sighed, the soft sound a small measure of irritation. "It's a simple donation, McAllister. It's for the society's annual benefit gala. We've always participated in the event and the society was instrumental in having the Saint Charles declared an historic landmark several years ago. The organizers are very old-monied New Orleanians. Most of them are clients of the hotel. I can assure you the hotel gets a fair return for the donation, not to mention some good press."

"It seems to me the hotel would have to get some pretty heavy bookings to make up for a donation of this size. Five thousand dollars is a lot of money."

"Five thousand dollars," Madeline repeated, her shock obvious. "It was supposed to be for five hundred."

"Not according to your budget."

She came around the desk in a flash. "Let me see that report." Madeline snatched the document from his hand.

"Help yourself." Chase stepped back slightly to give her access and watched as she began flipping through the pages. Taking advantage of the moment, he breathed in the delicate floral scent that she wore. Sunshine and roses, he decided and wondered when he had begun to find the smell of sunshine and roses so sexy.

Since it came wrapped in the package of Madeline Charbonnet. A package equipped with thorns, he reminded himself.

"I was right. It is only five hundred dollars. Look, it says so right here," she told him, pointing to the entry.

Chase leaned closer and made a show of studying the report. "So it is. My mistake."

Madeline looked up from the report and found Chase's face scant inches from her own. She stared at the scar along his chin, then moved her gaze to his mouth. Her heart thrummed in her chest as she remembered the feel of his mouth against her own. His eyes darkened. He drew his finger along the line of her jaw and she bit her bottom lip to keep it from quivering in response to his touch.

"Madeline," he whispered.

The sound of her name broke the spell and Madeline jerked away. *What had she been thinking of?* She swallowed hard, praying Chase hadn't noted her reaction. "Well, I guess I'd better get back to work."

She waited for Chase to step back so she could pass. When he didn't, she was forced to look at him again. Amusement flickered in his eyes, turning them to a rich shade of blue that reminded her of the sky on a clear spring day. A smile tugged at the corners of his lips.

Damn him. Madeline looked away. Despite her attempts to treat him with cool professionalism and indifference, he had known she was anything but indifferent to him. She cursed him again and then herself. Evidently she had masochistic tendencies, Madeline decided. Why else would she find that wicked smile of his so attractive?

"What about the tickets?"

"The tickets?" Madeline repeated, his question pulling her from her thoughts.

"For the Preservation Society Gala. Your report indicated the donation purchased tickets to the gala. Five hundred dollars per couple." He tapped his finger on the entry. "Since the hotel donated the five hundred dollars, I'm assuming you got the tickets."

"Actually, it's only one ticket that admits two people."

"And were you planning to use it?" Chase asked.

"As a matter of fact, I was," Madeline told him. "Is that a problem?"

"No. No problem. What time do we have to be there?"

Madeline's head shot up. Her eyes darted to his. "We?"

"Yes. As in you and me. I thought this would be a good opportunity to let you introduce me to some of the hotel's more discriminating clientele."

"Suppose I already have a date?" she challenged.

Leaning a fraction closer, Chase slid his finger down the lapel of her jacket. "Do you?"

Her stomach dipped at his nearness and the seductive tenor of his voice. Madeline clenched her hands into fists at her side to keep them from reaching out to touch him. She tipped up her chin. "No."

"Then there shouldn't be any problem. In your own words, it's for the benefit of the hotel." He continued to finger the lapel of her jacket. "And since it's a business expense paid for by the hotel and you and I both want to see the hotel succeed, it only makes sense that I be the one to go with you. Besides, this will be a good time for you to smooth the way for me in that elite little circle we discussed earlier."

Unnerved by his nearness, Madeline wanted to retreat from the contact. But one look at the amused gleam in his eyes and she dug in her heels. She wouldn't give him the satisfaction.

"Chin up, Princess. Just consider it part of your job."

"The hotel doesn't offer combat pay," she tossed back.

Chase laughed. "No. I guess you'll just have to settle for me as your date Saturday evening instead."

"My date," she repeated, her temper escalating by the second.

"That's right."

She flicked a pointed glance at his fingers on her lapel and Chase dropped his hand. She waited. When he finally stepped back, Madeline brushed past him. After stalking across the room, she whirled around to face him. "I suppose you think I should be flattered by this pathetic attempt of yours to get me to go out with you?"

"You thought it was pathetic? I didn't think it was pathetic. Transparent maybe. But then, I've already told you subtlety's not one of my virtues."

He grinned and Madeline hardened her heart to his rakish charm. "No, subtlety is not one of your virtues, Chase McAllister. Neither is fair play. I should have refused to justify those promotional expenses to you."

The smile on his lips faded. "You didn't have any choice, and you won't have one in the future either—not as long as I'm responsible for this hotel. Get used to it, Princess. Maybe you and your father didn't have to justify personal expenses charged to the hotel in the past, but you do now. In case you've forgotten, this is no longer your family's hotel."

Madeline glared at him. "How could I forget, when you keep reminding me every chance you get."

"Then let me also remind you that I'm the one in charge of this hotel."

"So you keep telling me."

"And I'm going to continue to tell you until I'm sure you understand exactly what that means."

"Oh, I understand what it means all right," she snapped, no longer able to control her temper. "It means you get to play lord of the manor. Is that the secret to your success with Majestic, McAllister? Flash your sexy little grin, kiss the females until they're dizzy, then bark out your orders and everyone obeys. Or maybe that's just the way you get your kicks. Either way, it's not going to work on me."

Chase flashed her that infernal grin. "I didn't know you found my grin sexy."

"I don't," she said and cursed herself for giving him this new ammunition.

"Do my kisses really make you dizzy, Princess?"

"No."

"Guess I'll have to work on that."

"Not with me you won't."

"Is that a dare? If it is, I should let you know, I've never been a fellow who could resist a dare. Sort of like waving a red flag in front of a bull kind of thing."

"Now why doesn't that surprise me? The idea of you and barnyard animals having something in common." If the jab bothered him, he certainly didn't show it.

"Nope, never could resist a dare," he continued, amusement lighting his eyes. "Back when I was in the boys' home, if one of the other guys dared me to climb the highest branch in the tree, I did it—no matter how scared I was."

"Sounds to me like you had a big ego even as a child." But her words no longer held any heat. The image of Chase as a lonely little boy took the zip out of her anger as nothing else could have.

"I did," he agreed, smiling. "Got me in lots of trouble, too. Why I remember the time one of the older kids dared me to drop a cherry bomb down the letter chute of the rectory."

"You didn't?"

"I did. And caught hell for it, too. But I couldn't walk away from the challenge. I still can't."

Madeline stiffened her spine. Challenge? Here she was feeling all sad and teary-eyed over him, and he was thinking of her as a challenge. "I'm not one of your juvenile challenges, McAllister."

"No, you're not." Chase moved his gaze over her slowly. Laughter danced in his eyes. "There's not anything remotely juvenile about you."

Madeline simmered. "You can save the smoldering looks for the poor females who find your brand of charm appealing."

"Which you don't."

"That's right. I don't."

"Another dare, Princess?" Chase asked softly. "I told you I'm not a man who can resist a dare."

"Don't flatter yourself, McAllister. I'm simply not interested."

"Not interested? Or could it be that you're simply afraid?"

Madeline rolled her eyes heavenward. "That ego of yours really is incredible. Evidently it's affected your hearing. So I'll repeat myself. *I am not interested.*"

"You know, I think I'm going to enjoy changing your mind."

Madeline started towards the door. "There's little chance of that."

"Why? Because you're immune to my sexy smile and, what did you call it? Oh, yeah. My smoldering looks?"

"Repulsed is more like it," she tossed over her shoulder before reaching for the doorknob.

Chase smacked his hand flat against the door, preventing her from opening it.

Madeline spun around, her heart pounding at the swiftness of his movements. She hadn't even heard him come up behind her, and now he was standing dangerously close, so close she could see the flecks of indigo in his eyes.

"Prove it," he whispered. "Go with me to the gala Saturday night."

Madeline hesitated.

"Going out with me shouldn't be a problem—unless, of course, you're not as immune to me as you claim."

"All right, McAllister," Madeline returned, taking up the gauntlet he had tossed at her feet. The man really did need to be taken down a peg or two, she reasoned. "It's black tie." She made a point of flicking her gaze over his rolled-up sleeves and tieless shirt. "I assume you can come up with a tux."

His lips twitched. "I think I can scrounge one up."

"Fine. Cocktails start at seven."

"I'll pick you up at six-thirty."

"No, *I'll* pick *you* up," she told him, flashing him a smug smile of her own. At the arch of his brow, she added, "It's the nineties, McAllister. I'd suggest you get with it."

"I've never had a date pick me up before," he replied, amusement coloring his voice.

"Sorry, but I'm not going to be the one to introduce you to dating in this century. Because this isn't a date. It's business."

Five

It's not a date. It's business. Madeline repeated the chant that she had invoked incessantly while dressing for this evening. Turning the wheel of her car, she aimed it in the direction of the hotel. So what if she had taken extra care in getting ready for tonight? It had nothing to do with Chase.

In a pig's eye it didn't.

For the past week she had been like a twittering schoolgirl getting ready for her first prom. The fact that she had gone out and bought a new dress, fussed over her makeup and even put her hair up were proof enough. Sighing, she tapped her fingers against the steering wheel and waited for the light to turn green. *Face it, Madeline. The man may have maneuvered you into going out with him tonight, but you allowed yourself to be maneuvered.*

There was no way of getting around it. Honesty compelled her to admit the truth—at least to herself. Deep down inside she was attracted to Chase McAllister on both a physical and an emotional level. She didn't like it. She certainly hadn't planned on this complication when she had decided to stay on at the hotel and try to win the assistant GM position. She had been determined to hate him, to find fault with the way he operated the hotel. After all, he and his firm had in essence snatched her dream from her. But in all fairness, she couldn't hate him. He worked just as hard as she did, and with the exception of her father, he had managed to charm the entire hotel staff.

Including her.

Maybe it was that brief glimpse he had given her into his childhood. The tender way he had spoken of his mother had stirred something inside her and made it impossible to hate him. Whatever the reason, and despite his cocksure attitude, she liked Chase McAllister.

And what was worse, she wanted him. His kisses left her light-headed. His touch made her ache for things she had no business thinking of. Remembering the feel of his mouth hot and hungry against her own, Madeline clenched the steering wheel and drew a deep breath. The fact that Chase made no secret of his desire for her made resisting him even more difficult. For the first time in her life she found herself tempted to engage in what would surely be a casual affair. Besides, even if it weren't for his imminent departure in a few months, Chase wasn't the sort of man to put down roots physically or emotionally. Now that she thought of it, that was probably why he was so successful at his job. Working for a company like Majestic suited him. The constant shifting from property to property catered to his gypsy life-style.

And smacked of no commitments, no strings—something she deemed essential to any relationship. She had no choice but to continue to keep him at arm's length. But, recalling the heat in his eyes, the husky timbre of his voice when he told her he would see her tonight, Madeline's pulse skittered.

Disgusted with her reaction, she hit the gas pedal as the light turned green and sent the car forward with a jerk. Moments later when she pulled the car up in front of the hotel, she buoyed herself with the knowledge that she was the one who would set the tone for the evening. After all, she was the one in the driver's seat. Hence, she was the one in charge.

"Evening, Ms. Charbonnet." The valet opened her car door.

"Good evening, Simon. Don't park it. I'll only be a minute," she informed him as she exited the car.

Taking another deep breath, Madeline unclenched her fingers and strode into the hotel. Quickly she scanned the lobby where she had instructed Chase to meet her, but there was no sign of him. Suddenly her victory at being the one to pick him up tonight lost some of its flavor. Given the gossip-prone nature of the hotel, she didn't want the employees to misconstrue the two of them going out together. Going to his room to find him would only be grist for the gossip mill. So would having the desk clerk call to announce her arrival. Silently Madeline cursed Chase.

"Madeline, is that you?"

Madeline bit back a groan before turning her attention to the night manager behind the front desk. "Hi, Janet. And yes, it's me."

"That's some dress," the other woman told her.

Flushing, Madeline chastised herself for giving in to temptation and buying the dress. Made of soft crepe, the design had been deceptively simple on the hanger with its long sleeves and off-the-shoulder neckline. But when she had slipped it on, she had fallen in love with it. Baring the tops of her shoulders and back, the fabric gently cupped her curves and skimmed dangerously high along her thighs. The deep green color had done wonderful things for her eyes and skin. It didn't matter that every ounce she ate would probably be visible in the clinging little number. She had felt wickedly feminine and sexy in the outfit and had been unable to resist it.

"I take it you're not here to work."

"No, I'm not. I'm here to pick up... to meet Chase. Mr. McAllister," she amended. "We have a business engagement." But from the other woman's expression, Madeline doubted she believed her. Blast the man. She had told him to meet her in the lobby. The last thing she wanted or needed was speculation among the staff about them.

"Want me to ring his room?"

Just then the elevator gave a little ping and the doors slid open. Out walked Chase.

"Wow," Janet said.

Wow was right, Madeline thought. Her stomach did another flutter kick as he walked toward her. She had found him attractive in a suit. Even in a wrinkled shirt with the cuffs rolled up to his elbows and his tie mangled he had been attractive. But Chase McAllister in black tie and tux was devastating.

"Looks like I owe that guy in the men's store an apology. Judging from the way that sassy little mouth of yours is hanging open, the price of this getup was worth every penny he charged me."

Madeline clamped her mouth shut. "You were supposed to be down here for six-forty," she told him, irritated with herself for allowing him to catch her drooling over him like a lovesick adolescent. "You're late."

"You know, Princess, you're the only woman I know who's such a stickler about time. Are you always so punctual?"

"Always."

He laughed. "What do you know? A woman after my own heart."

Ignoring him, Madeline started for the lobby doors. "I'm parked out front."

"Wait a minute." Chase caught her arm, halting her progression. She turned to look at him. "Aren't you forgetting something?"

"Like what?" she asked, frowning.

"My flowers."

"Your flowers," she repeated dumbfounded. "Why on earth would I bring you flowers?"

Laughter danced in his blue eyes. "Because I'm your date, and when I take a woman out for a fancy evening I generally bring her flowers."

Madeline glared at him. "Funny, McAllister. Real funny."

"Hey, I'm a nineties guy," he told her as he followed her outside to the car.

The valet held open the passenger door for Madeline, clearly expecting her to allow Chase to drive. She ignored the gesture and walked around to the driver's seat. Chase's chuckle when she slid behind the wheel and buckled her seat belt only added to her irritation.

With Chase seated beside her, her sleek, red Mercedes-Benz seemed suddenly much smaller. His scent, an appealing blend of spice and soap, lingered in the confining space, making her keenly aware of his presence.

"Nice dress," Chase told her, breaking the tense silence.

"Thanks." She had no intention of telling him how good he looked, not when her open-mouthed gawking had done so already.

"I half expected you to show up in another one of those suits you always wear. I'm glad you didn't."

Madeline frowned again. "What's wrong with my suits?"

"Nothing. Incidentally, the red one's my favorite."

Don't bite, Madeline told herself. *Don't let him pull you in.* But after a few seconds she couldn't resist. "Why the red one?" she asked him warily, not quite sure she would like the answer, but wanting it just the same.

"It has the shortest skirt."

She cut him a disapproving glance meant to take him down a peg. It had no effect on him. "I guess I should have expected a sexist comment like that from you."

"What can I say? I like looking at your legs. You have great legs, Princess."

She could feel his gaze slide over her and Madeline bit back the urge to tug on the dress's hem. Instead, she concentrated on steering the Mercedes into the lane for valet parking.

"Madeline?"

When she didn't respond, he cupped her chin gently and turned her to face him. Her stomach did another twist at the dark look in his eyes.

And then he was kissing her, his mouth brushing tenderly across her own. Her eyes fluttered shut as his tongue skimmed lazily across her lips, drugging her with his taste, his touch. She opened her mouth to him. Her body hummed when his tongue met hers and twined. Wanting, needing to be closer, she reached out to touch him.

And the car jolted forward. Madeline jerked back, but already Chase was shoving the gear shift into park. Mortified that she had so completely lost control, Madeline wrapped her fingers around the steering wheel and squeezed her eyes shut. She couldn't look at him, not now. Not after coming apart in his arms.

"Relax, Princess. So we got a little carried away. That's no reason for you to be so upset and let it ruin our first date."

"I am not upset and this isn't a date. It's business," she managed to say over the thickness in her throat.

"It certainly feels like a date to me."

"Well it isn't." She opened her eyes and looked straight ahead, irritated with him for his speedy recovery, when her body still buzzed with desire.

"I really do like that dress."

"You've already said that." Shifting gears, she inched the car a little closer to the entrance.

"Yeah, I know. But I didn't tell you what I liked most about it."

"No doubt, the length," she informed him dryly.

"Yeah, that, too," he said, amusement coloring his voice. "But what I like most is the prospect of getting you out of it."

The valet attendant opening her car door saved Madeline from answering. A good thing, she decided as she hurried up the steps to the hotel, because she wasn't at all sure she could speak.

The few minutes it took to reach the ballroom seemed like an eternity with Chase walking beside her. After handing in their invitation at the door, Madeline stepped into the room.

Two dozen tables draped in silver lamé cloths had been arranged to form an arc around the marble dance floor. Stems of fuchsia-and-white irises mixed with freesia and sprigs of green foliage spilled from crystal vases and reflected in mirrored tiles that lined the center of the silver cloths. Music mingled with the clink of crystal and laughter as two hundred of the city's most prominent citizens shimmered and smiled in their jewels and finery.

"Fancy crowd," Chase remarked from beside her.

"Yes, it is." Madeline looked out at the people, seeing the familiar faces. Bankers, doctors, millionaire philanthropists. Not a single one of them made her as nervous as the man standing next to her. "We'll need to check the seating chart to find out where our table is," Madeline told him, indicating the diagrams set up against the wall.

"I'll check on it, if you promise not to run away the minute I leave you alone."

For the first time since they had kissed in the car Madeline looked at him. Her spine stiffened at the smug expression on his face. "And what makes you think I'm going to run away?"

His lips curved into that wicked smile. "Princess, you and I both know the answer to that. I want you, and you're scared silly because you want me, too."

She wanted to call him a liar, but couldn't. It was true. She did want him and it scared her—not that she would admit it to him. Instead she quipped, "Put that ego of yours in check, McAllister, and go find out where we're supposed to be sitting."

Once he started off in the direction of the seating charts, Madeline made an effort to regain a measure of control.

"Madeline, dear. How lovely it is to see you."

"Hello, Mrs. Bouvier." Madeline smiled at the chairwoman of the Preservation Society. From a prominent New Orleans family, Mignon Bouvier had retained much of the beauty that had attracted so many suitors during her debutante days forty years earlier. Wealthy and well connected socially, the woman held the power to send bookings worth thousands of dollars to the Saint Charles. But as yet, Madeline had been unable to get her into the hotel, let alone convince her to use their services. "How are you?"

"I'm just fine, dear. We were so glad the Saint Charles was able to continue to support the society."

"We wouldn't think of not participating," Chase said as he came up behind Madeline. "Hello, Mrs. Bouvier."

"Why Mr. McAllister. We...that is, the society didn't realize you would be attending our little gala." The woman practically fluttered.

"Madeline persuaded me to come. And I must say, now that I'm here, I'm glad she did."

Persuaded him? The man had insisted on coming despite her protests. Madeline had to bite back the urge to call him on the fib. From the mocking gleam in his eyes, he knew it, too.

"It's been quite a while since I've seen you and your husband at the Saint Charles."

Mrs. Bouvier blushed. "We've both been very busy, but I promise we'll come in next week for dinner."

Madeline couldn't believe it. The woman actually preened under Chase's attention. Fascinated, she watched the exchange play out.

"I'll be sure to let André know to expect you," Chase continued. "I'll have him reserve you a table in the garden room when you call."

After bidding Mignon Bouvier goodbye, they began weaving their way across the room towards the tables. "That was smooth, McAllister."

"I thought so."

"Do you realize who she is?"

Chase caught her hand and placed it on his arm. "Mignon Claiborne Bouvier, wife of Charles S. Bouvier, Chairman of the Board of Bouvier Financial. A patron of the arts, she and her husband have a private art collection on loan to the New Orleans Museum of Art that is estimated to be worth in the neighborhood of ten million. Philanthropists devoted to education, each year they bestow several sizable endowments to the city's major universities. Besides being among the wealthiest and most influential members of the community, they each hold seats on the boards of the city's two largest universities.''

"You've done your homework," Madeline told him, impressed. "I suppose you also know that the Saint Charles has been courting them, trying to secure the room nights and catering business for those universities' open houses and homecomings this fall."

"And the Saint Charles is going to get it."

"You sound pretty sure of yourself," she told him.

"No, Princess. It's you I'm sure of. You'll get the account."

Surprised by his answer, Madeline remained silent, but was unable to suppress the pleasure his words gave her.

The music stopped and the emcee for the evening moved to the microphone. "Ladies and gentlemen, if you will please find your seats. We have a lovely evening planned for you and..."

"What's our table number?" she asked Chase.

"Thirteen."

Thirteen, she thought, biting her lip. She could only pray it wasn't a sign of bad things to come. So far the evening and her time with Chase was not going at all as she had expected. Instead of putting distance between them, she found herself being drawn further under his spell.

Chase patted her hand. "Don't worry. Thirteen's my lucky number." Those eyes of hers really were a dead giveaway to her feelings, Chase thought as he guided her through the tables. Right now she looked vulnerable, triggering some primal urge in him to hold her close and comfort her.

Not a good idea, McAllister. He wouldn't be content with just holding her and neither would she. He had seen the shock in those big green eyes earlier. She had been rocked by the kiss they'd shared and mortified by her own response. He would have been gratified by her reaction if he hadn't been so staggered by his own response. When she had opened her mouth to him and flicked her tongue against his, he had nearly lost it. Never before had desire held such a stranglehold over him. She hadn't been the only one who had lost sense of time and place. Were it not for the car jerking forward when she had removed her foot from the brake...

"Something wrong?" Madeline asked.

"No." Nothing except that just thinking about making love to Madeline had him growing hard.

"There's table thirteen," Madeline told him, releasing his arm to precede him.

"Well it's about time you got here," a petite but very pregnant brunette announced.

"Chloe, what are you doing here? I thought you and Paul decided not to come."

The other woman wrinkled her nose. "You mean Paul the Dictator decided an evening of good food and dancing would be too much for me and the baby. But I'm happy to say I was able to convince him otherwise." Her attention shifted from Madeline to Chase. "Well, well, well," she said, her dark eyes twinkling with curiosity.

"Oh, I'm sorry." Madeline turned to Chase. "Chloe James this is—"

"The hunk."

Chase chuckled and offered his hand. "Chase McAllister, Mrs. James. It's a pleasure."

"Oh, the pleasure's mine. And please, call me Chloe and I'll call you Chase. I've heard so much about you, I feel as though I already know you."

Chase quirked his brow in question.

"Madeline's mentioned your name a time or two."

"Is that so?" He cut a glance to Madeline who was glaring at her friend. "I trust it wasn't all bad."

Chloe laughed, earning another scowl from Madeline. "No, not all of it. As a matter of fact, she hasn't referred to you as a jerk in over a week."

"Then I suppose I'm making some progress," Chase said, his eyes locking on Madeline.

She steadfastly avoided his gaze. "Chloe, where's Paul?"

"Trying to round up some Perrier and lemon for me." She patted her round stomach. "The tyrant won't even allow me to have a teeny sip of wine."

"Because it's not good for the baby. Here's your Perrier, darling," a man said from behind her. Slightly taller than Chase's own six feet, Paul James had the same dark hair and eyes as his wife. Smiling he extended his hand. "Paul James, otherwise known as the tyrant."

Chase laughed as they shook hands, warming to the other man immediately. "Chase McAllister, otherwise known as the jerk and the hunk, depending on who you ask."

"Ah, so you're Madeline's new boss."

"Yes." And with some luck he hoped to soon be her lover.

"I think we'd better sit down," Madeline informed them primly. "The waiters are bringing out the salads now."

"Well, I for one am starved," Chloe informed them as they took their seats.

"Darling, you've *stayed* hungry since you got pregnant," her husband teased.

"That's because I'm eating for two," Chloe responded. "Does anyone know what's on the menu for tonight?"

"Fish and prime rib," Madeline advised them. She looked across the table at Chase. "The chef here does an excellent job with the fish. You might want to try it."

"Maybe some other time. Tonight I'm feeling rather carnivorous."

But more than two hours later, the meal had done little to take the edge off of his hunger—because the hunger gnawing inside him had nothing to do with food and everything to do with Madeline. The sax wailed with a soft, bluesy note and Chase guided her in a turn as they danced beneath the crystal chandelier. His cheek brushed the wisps of hair that trailed along the sides of her face and down her neck. Even her hair carried that delicate floral scent that he had begun to associate with her. He wondered, yet again, when the scent of roses had become a source of erotic fantasies for him.

The music played on, wrapping him in its sultry sounds. Madeline's body swayed in rhythm with his, and Chase pulled her a fraction closer. He bit back a moan at the feel of her breasts pressed intimately against him, her legs moving in and out between his own as she mirrored his steps.

If Madeline had thought dancing would ease the sexual tension her friend Chloe's matchmaking attempts had engendered, then her plan had backfired miserably—at least as far as he was concerned. Her hip shifted innocently against him, increasing his torture. Whoever had invented the first slow dance had obviously done so with mating in mind, Chase decided. Because making love to Madeline was definitely first and foremost in his thoughts.

He brushed his mouth against the delicate shell of her ear. She trembled, sending a violent surge of desire through him. "Madeline—"

"It's getting late. I think it's time we get going. I have a busy day tomorrow, and I'm sure you do, too." She stepped back out of his arms and started off the dance floor, but Chase didn't miss the breathless tone of her voice.

He caught her arm to slow her flight and took her hand in his. "Tomorrow's Sunday," he reminded her. "You've got the day off."

"But the hotel doesn't. And I have some paperwork to catch up on."

Taking satisfaction in the fact that the pulse was as unsteady as his own, Chase didn't argue as he led her back to the table and said their goodbyes.

Minutes later when the valet pulled the red Mercedes up in front of the hotel, Chase opened the passenger door. "I'll drive," he told her. After a moment's hesitation, Madeline slid into the seat. He slipped some bills into the valet's hand and eased behind the wheel of the car.

In the confines of the car, her scent wafted around him, doing nothing to ease the ache in his body that had begun the moment he had seen her at the hotel.

"I didn't realize you were actually considering the conference center addition for the hotel," Madeline interjected into the silence.

"It was a good suggestion on your part. I think you were right. The hotel needs it if we're going to compete for the convention business. I'd be foolish if I didn't at least look into it."

"Paul's a good architect. It was nice of you to offer him an opportunity to bid on the work," she told him.

Chase shrugged. "I'll still have to run the numbers before Majestic's board. But if his work is as good as he says and the price is right, he'll be the one doing me a favor. I wasn't looking forward to interviewing a half dozen other firms. Besides, I liked him. I liked both of your friends." He paused and slanted a glance toward her. Moonlight streamed in through the window, bathing her face in soft light that gave her skin a pale glow. His gazed drifted to her bare shoulders where the light spilled across the swell of her breasts outlined by the stretch of dark fabric. Desire stirred and twisted in his gut as he contemplated the feel of that moon-kissed skin beneath his hands. He lifted his gaze to meet hers.

Madeline swallowed and looked away to stare out the window. "They're good people. I've known Chloe since kindergarten and Paul—"

"Madeline."

"Yes?"

"I'm not interested in making small talk about your friends or the hotel. And I don't think you are, either."

She fell silent, and he turned his attention back to the road as he guided the sleek car through the dark streets. But even without looking, he sensed her nervousness as she sat in the seat beside him. He turned off the main thoroughfare in the direction of Madeline's home.

"You've turned the wrong way," Madeline said, her voice slightly alarmed. "The hotel's in the other direction."

"I'm not going to the hotel. I'm taking you home."

"No!"

The single word held a wealth of panic that had Chase shifting his gaze to her. "Why not?"

"Because you won't have a way to get back to the hotel."

"I can take a taxi. Or," he said, smiling, "you could invite me to spend the night with you."

"In your dreams, McAllister."

"Yeah. There, too. I've spent quite a few nights fantasizing what it's going to be like between us when we finally do make love."

"Well, you can just keep on fantasizing because it's never going to happen."

Chase pulled the car into her driveway and cut the engine. Turning to Madeline, he reached out and fingered the wispy curls that whispered along her neck. He leaned closer, bringing his lips to within a fraction of hers. "Isn't it?"

Confusion and alarm registered in her sea green eyes, and then suddenly she was jerking away. Fumbling with the seat belt, she unsnapped it and raced from the car to the house.

"We need to talk, Madeline," Chase told her when he joined her at the doorway.

"There's nothing to talk about."

"Isn't there?" Taking the key from her hand, he unlocked the door of the Victorian-style cottage and followed her inside before she could close the door in his face.

She moved across the room, flipping on lamp switches. "You can use the phone in the living room to call a taxi," she told him.

Her prim and proper tone rankled, making him want to put a chink in that cool veneer. She set her evening bag down on the bar, and when she turned around, he was waiting. "Sooner or later you're going to have to face it, Princess."

He was so close Madeline could see the tiny jagged design in the scar on his chin, marking where the stitches had been. "I don't know what you're talking about," she lied, hating that faint quaver in her voice.

He moved slowly, slipping his hands around her waist and pulling her to fit against him. "I'm talking about this," he murmured before settling his mouth against hers.

He kissed her leisurely, as though he wanted to explore and savor every angle of her mouth. Her pulse tap-danced as his tongue slipped between her lips and mated with her own. He tasted like danger—dark and wild and forbidden. And sent desire speeding through her like a lightning bolt.

She clutched at his shoulders, curling her fists in his jacket. He inched his fingers up along her waist, her sides, beneath the curve of her breasts. Madeline's heart pounded. When he brushed his thumbs across her nipples, her breath snagged in her throat and she whimpered.

"Lord, I want you," he said against her mouth in a voice husky with arousal. "Where's your bedroom?"

"No," she said, pressing her palms against his shoulders before he could kiss her again. She wondered where she had found the strength to stop, when she wanted so much more.

"We want each other. It's not going to go away just because you're afraid."

"I'm not afraid," she countered, hiking her chin up a notch.

He caught her trembling fingers and brought them to his lips. He kissed them. "Aren't you? You've been running scared since the first time I kissed you."

Madeline sighed. She hated the fact that he was right. "It would be foolish of me not to admit that I'm attracted to you when obviously I am. And while I'm sure that sex with you would be a...a momentous experience, I don't indulge in casual sex, Chase."

"I didn't think you did. For the record, neither do I. So what's the problem?"

"The problem is you'll be gone in a few months."

"All the more reason we shouldn't waste time now." He started to tug her closer.

"No." Madeline pulled her hands free and moved away from him, needing space and distance to clear her head. "I can't think clearly when you're touching me."

He gave her that wicked smile.

"Wipe that grin off your face, McAllister."

"Sorry." But he didn't look the least bit sorry. "How about if I kiss you again and see if that helps you make up your mind."

She glared at him. Oh, the rat was enjoying this. "Here." She held out the keys to her car. "How about you take yourself on back to the hotel now, and I'll let you know if I change my mind."

He hesitated for long moments, then reached for the keys, tugging her hand and pulling her to him. He kissed her again, long and thoroughly, stoking the fires, making her cling to him as her knees turned to jelly.

When he lifted his head, he whispered, "Oh, you'll change your mind, Princess. Count on it. In the meantime, I'm going to see to it that you have a lot more trouble thinking clearly."

Six

―――――

Madeline stepped off the elevator. Her heels sank in the plush carpet as she walked determinedly down the corridor leading to the suite of executive offices. It had been more than a week since Chase had accompanied her to the Preservationist Society's gala. After kissing her senseless and boldly declaring he wanted to make love to her, he had jetted off to Majestic's corporate offices back East, leaving her heart and her body a war of muddled emotions. She knew from her father's grumblings and the hotel grapevine that he had returned two nights ago, but as yet she hadn't seen him.

The old adage "Out of sight, out of mind" was definitely not true, Madeline decided. Because she had thought of little else but Chase since he had left her cottage. Even her father's continual complaints about Chase and rejoicing at his absence had done little to dim the tug of desire his kisses had set off inside her.

And she was no closer to a making a decision about him now than she had been a week ago. If anything, she was even

more confused. Recalling the touch of his hands, the taste
of his mouth, a shiver ran through her and Madeline quickened her pace. It was chemistry, sex, she told herself. She
sighed. No matter how she defined it, she wanted him.
There was no getting around it. She knew all the reasons not
to become involved with him. She had gone over them in her
head a hundred times already. A man like Chase knew the
effect he had on women. He probably changed lovers the
way other men changed their socks. A relationship with him
would have no future. He was only here temporarily.

Then why was she seriously considering going to bed with
him? Pausing outside the door leading to the suite of executive offices, Madeline dragged her fingers through her hair.
Did he expect an answer to his offer that they have an affair? Was that the reason he had sent for her? And if he took
her in his arms, kissed her and asked her again, would she
have the strength to say no?

Bracing herself, Madeline opened the door with unsteady fingers. She scanned the room for his secretary.
Grateful to find it empty, she sank down on the chair and
drew a deep breath while she tried to clear her jumbled
thoughts.

What was the matter with her? An affair with Chase was
out of the question. She couldn't do it, had been crazy to
even consider it. Granted, she was attracted to him. Despite her efforts not to, she liked him, probably more than
she should. But that was no reason to hop into bed with the
man. Besides, an affair would only complicate things, and
she didn't need or want any more complications in her life.
Her answer was no. It had to be.

Agitated, Madeline stood. She squared her shoulders. She
would simply tell Chase "Thanks but no thanks." No doubt
he would give up on her and move on to more willing game.
The thought brought a swift pang to her chest, but Madeline shoved it aside and started for his office. Finding the
door ajar, she raised her hand to knock, but paused at the
sound of a woman's sobbing. She started to retreat, then
stopped.

"Oh, Mr. Chase, I don't know what to say," the woman managed between sobs.

"Don't say anything, Ruthie. You just take this and go on home and get some rest. Spend some time with your family. And I don't want to see you back here until the doctor says you're well."

Ruthie Boudreaux. Madeline recognized the voice of one of the hotel's waitresses. Although only in her late thirties, Ruthie looked older than her years. With five children at home and a husband out of work, Madeline had suspected she was having a rough time financially when she had asked to work extra shifts. She had even worried that the woman was running herself down. But when she had tried suggesting that Ruthie slow down, the other woman had insisted she was fine and pleaded that her extra shifts not be cut. Madeline's father had instructed her not to interfere when she had confided her concerns.

Evidently Chase had decided to interfere.

"But this is your personal check. I can't take money from you, Mr. Chase. I can't accept charity. My Albert may not have a job right now, but he's a proud man."

"I know and please, it's not charity. It...I would consider it a favor to me if you would accept it, Ruthie." He paused. "You see, my mother was a waitress, too. She worked hard just like you do and she really liked her job. But I remember times when she wasn't feeling well, or I would come down with a bug and want her to stay home with me. Only, she couldn't for the same reason you didn't. Because getting paid for the sick day wasn't enough. She needed the tips, too. I wasn't able to help my mother then, and she's dead now so there's nothing I can do for her. So, please," he said, his voice husky. "Allow me to help you the way I wanted to help her."

Madeline's throat grew dry, and she swallowed hard against the thickness of tears.

"Seeing's how you put it like that. All right. I'll take it. But still it just don't seem right. I mean it being your personal check and all."

"It's right if I say it is. Haven't you heard? I'm the boss around here."

The other woman chuckled, but the laughter faded as she said, "You're a good man, Mr. Chase. I don't know how I'll pay you back, but I will somehow. I promise. As soon as my Albert finds himself another job."

"Don't worry about paying me back. Consider it a bonus for sneaking me all those extra blueberry muffins. Now you go home and get yourself well. Those children need you, and the hotel needs you—but not before you're ready to come back."

Blinking back tears, Madeline moved away from the door. She didn't want to embarrass Ruthie by letting her know that she had overheard her conversation with Chase. And she didn't want to face Chase right now—not when her heart was feeling so full. She would come back later, she told herself, when she was feeling less emotional. But as she started to leave, the door to the suite opened.

"Mr. McAllister wants files set up for each of the equipment contracts," Chase's secretary told the clerk who followed her into the executive offices. Spotting Madeline, she smiled. "Hi, Madeline. Does Chase know you're here?"

"No," Madeline managed to respond. "I just got here a few minutes ago. And I think he has someone with him."

"Well, he shouldn't be much longer. Let me get Susie started on these files, and then I'll buzz through and tell him you're here."

"Take your time," Madeline told her as the other woman gathered stacks of folders and papers and led Susie into an adjoining office.

When she was alone once more, Madeline walked over to the window and looked down over the busy street. A lone streetcar lumbered down the center of the avenue along metal tracks that had worn well with age. Cars flanked the trolley on both sides, zipping up and down the paved street. Madeline stared out at the symbols of past and present, but her thoughts were on the man in the other room.

Darn you, Chase McAllister. Things would have been so much simpler if you had kept on being the jerk I'd thought you were. Why did you have to be such a nice guy to Ruthie? Why did you have to make me care about you?

"Thanks again, Mr. Chase."

Madeline swiped at the corner of her eyes as she heard Ruthie exiting Chase's office.

"Don't forget. You have Albert come see me. The hotel always needs somebody who knows a thing or two about old equipment. That temperamental boiler's cost me more than one good dress shirt."

Madeline somehow managed to acknowledge Ruthie, and once the woman was gone, she went in. Chase stood at the center of the room in slate-colored slacks and white dress shirt. For once his tie was in place, even if his jacket was missing. He smiled at her, warmth and welcome in his eyes. All her determination to keep her distance, to end things between them before they got started, crumbled like the dust from a piece of pottery left too long in the sun. She went to him, cupped his face in her hands and kissed him gently on the mouth. "Thank you," she whispered.

Sliding his arms around her waist, Chase nuzzled her neck. "Not that I'm complaining, but if you tell me exactly what is it I'm being thanked for, I'll try to do it again."

She heard the smile in his voice, and it fed the warmth in her heart. "For being kind and generous. For caring about Ruthie and her family."

He stopped the nuzzling and drew back to look at her. "Eavesdropping, Princess? You?"

"Yes," Madeline admitted, seeing no point in lying. "I didn't mean to, and I know I shouldn't have, but I did."

He favored her with that cocky grin that she had begun to grow fond of. "Imagine that. A proper Southern lady like yourself listening at keyholes."

"Not at keyholes, McAllister. You left your door open." But Madeline couldn't help herself, she grinned at the laughter in his eyes.

Suddenly his lighthearted expression grew sober. "Lord, you look good. Even better than I remembered. And you smell good, too." He pulled her against him; his fingers slid into her hair and caressed her scalp. "Like roses and rain and hot sex on a moonlit beach."

Madeline's pulse stammered at the images his words evoked. Heat sliced through her, like that first and only shot of straight whiskey she'd sampled in her teens, burning a path straight to her core.

The sound of voices drifted to her and Madeline heard footsteps approaching. "Come on," Chase commanded, his voice a husky growl as he grabbed her hand and pulled her into his office. He shut the door and reached for her. "How about if I let you thank me again."

"No, don't." Madeline held up her hands to keep him at bay. "Please, Chase. Don't touch me. I told you I can't think when you're touching me." She hated the breathless tone of her voice almost as much as she hated making the admission.

"Princess, if that's supposed to discourage me, it isn't working." He tucked a strand of hair behind her ear, allowing his fingers to linger against her skin. Madeline's pulse stammered, and he gave her that infuriating smile again. "I like knowing I can scramble your brain."

She batted his hand away. "Well, I don't." She moved into the center of the office and out of his reach, keenly aware of those blue eyes of his tracking her progress.

"So where does that leave us?"

"I don't know," she admitted. "My feelings haven't changed, Chase. I want you. It scares me just how much I do want you. But you're moving too fast for me. I'm not used to this sort of thing. I can't just hop into bed with you because you turn me on."

"If it's what we both want, why not?"

Was the man being deliberately obtuse? "Because there are other things that need to be taken into consideration."

"Like what?"

"Like the fact that we have to work together and how a personal relationship between us might affect the hotel. And then there's my father. He—"

"Leave your father and the hotel out of this, Madeline. What's between us has nothing to do with them," he said, his voice hard, his eyes even harder. "This has to do with you and me. It has to do with sex. My wanting you and you wanting me." He shoved his hand through his hair. When he looked at her again, the darkness had dissolved. "Listen, you said I was moving too fast. Are you telling me you need more time? Is that it?"

"Yes. No. Maybe."

Grinning at her reply, Chase crossed the room and slipped his arms around her. "Want me to help you make up your mind?"

"You're scrambling my brain again, McAllister." She let out a long breath and allowed herself the pleasure of his embrace. "I told myself I was going to tell you to forget it. I wouldn't have an affair with you."

He stroked her back, sending tingles of pleasure and anticipation down her spine. "And now?"

"Now I'm not sure."

"All right."

"All right?" she repeated, confused by his response and a shade fearful that he had decided to move on to more willing game, just as she had predicted.

"I'll turn the heat down a notch and give you time to get used to the idea."

Madeline pulled back a fraction so she could see his face. "You make it sound like our becoming lovers is a given."

"It is as far as I'm concerned. But I'm willing to do some backpedaling until you get comfortable with the idea."

"That ego of yours is showing again, McAllister."

"It's a curse," he said, enjoying the sudden flash of fire in her green eyes.

"Well while you're doing that backpedaling, I suggest that *you* get comfortable with the idea that my answer might still be no."

He paused, giving consideration to that possibility. He didn't like it. He had truly missed her this past week, and he wasn't a man given to missing people or places. That had been another lesson he had learned at St. Mark's. Never let yourself become attached to people. Never let yourself get too comfortable and think of a place as home. Because sooner or later if the people didn't send you packing, the system would.

But he *had* missed Madeline, had chafed at being back in his own office in New Jersey. There was no other explanation for the way his thoughts had kept wandering to her. Thinking of how she managed to look both sexy and prim in her militant little suits. Of the way her eyes mirrored everything she was feeling. And judging from the way she was staring at him now, she found his silence disconcerting. "Okay," he said finally. "I'll accept the fact that you might decide against us going to bed together, as long as you accept the fact that I'm going to do my best to get you there."

She narrowed her eyes. "You said you'd back off and give me a chance to make up my mind."

Moving in slowly, he smiled as she stepped back and her bottom connected with the mahogany desk. "I said I'd turn down the heat. Not turn it off. How about if we settle on simmer?" Not waiting for her answer, he brushed his lips across hers. He heard her soft gasp, felt the quick shudder run through her as he sought entrance to her mouth. Heat sliced through him at her response. Pulling her closer, he deepened the kiss.

Her tongue met his, teased and danced in a mating ritual that turned his blood to lava and made the ache in his loins grow even more painful. Fighting for control, Chase lifted his head and gulped in fresh air.

"If that's your idea of simmer," she whispered, her voice shaky, "I don't want to see full boil."

It pleased him to see her take a few deep breaths of her own. "Then I'll try for simmer again," he promised and started to lower his head.

"No." She held up her hand. "Back off, McAllister, and give me some breathing room."

Chase didn't bother hiding his grin as he stepped away and allowed her to escape. Folding his arms, he leaned against the desk and waited while she smoothed her hair and the lines of her suit.

Her fingers stilled when she glanced up and realized he was watching her. "I should get back to work."

"Wait." Chase came away from the desk and followed her to the door. "I haven't had a chance to talk to you yet, to tell you why I sent for you."

Madeline hesitated.

"Come back and sit down." He returned to his desk and dropped into his chair. "I promise this is strictly business. I want to tell you about the outcome of my meetings with the Majestic board."

Madeline followed and took the seat across from him. She tilted her head and waited.

Chase leaned forward, eager to share the good news. "I gave them your proposal, outlining the need and the positive impact a conference center addition would mean to the hotel. I gave them a copy of your memo to me explaining how the conference center would allow the hotel to aggressively compete for a larger share of the convention business. They were very impressed, Madeline." Pleasure flooded him at the glow in her eyes, taking some of the edge off his desire for her. Strange, that seeing her happy could make him feel this good. "They took a vote and agreed to the addition. You're going to get your conference center, Madeline."

"I know," she said smiling. "My father told me last night."

His sudden burst of pleasure died at her words. Of course her father would tell her, Chase reasoned, scuffling to temper his disappointment. But *he* had wanted to be the one to give her the news and resented the other man for beating him to it.

"It's wonderful news, Chase. Just wonderful. Thank you so much."

Chase shrugged, his excitement lost at having his surprise for Madeline ruined by her father's early announcement. "Thank yourself, Princess. Your proposal was solid. I simply delivered the idea."

"I don't believe it. A sudden attack of modesty from Chase McAllister?" She laughed. "You did more than deliver it, Chase. According to my father, when they got him on the phone for the vote and he launched into his spiel for the conference center, you backed him up. He said you rammed the statistics down the board members' throats until they voted the way you wanted them to."

He had been heavy-handed, Chase admitted silently. He had wanted the conference center addition for the hotel—not only because it made good business sense, but because he knew it would please Madeline. So, he had thrown his weight as a partner and Majestic's troubleshooter around the boardroom table long before her father had been contacted by phone for his vote. Resentment tore through him as he thought of Henri refusing to attend the meeting because of his busy schedule.

"Thank you." She reached over and squeezed his hand.

Chase looked down at the small slender fingers that rested against his own, recalling how he had lain awake at night thinking of her, wanting her. Desire ripped through him again, staggering him with its intensity. He closed his fingers around hers.

Madeline paused, and as though sensing his shift in mood, she pulled back her hand. "It's going to mean a lot to the long-range future for the Saint Charles. I appreciate your getting the board to agree to the addition, Chase. My father and I both do."

Irritated by the mention of her father again, Chase stood. He paced the length of the room, stopping near the window. "If Paul James comes through with a good price, they should be able to start construction within a couple of weeks. With a little luck, you'll be able to start selling meeting space for the fall. You may want to start working with marketing on some brochures.''

''I'll do that,'' she said, her lips curving into a tentative smile. ''I've already come up with several ideas.''

Chase glanced over at her, sitting in the chair, her face glowing with excitement as she talked about her marketing ideas for the conference center and the positive impact it would have on the hotel. She belongs here, he thought, thinking how perfect she looked amidst the exquisite furnishings. The plush almond carpet, the drapes made of wine-colored damask, the antique settee and the framed Matisse resting above it—every inch of the place shouted class—just like Madeline.

And she'll be devastated when her father manages to lose it. He was crazy to do it, but he had to warn her. ''This is going to be an expensive project, Princess.''

''I know. My father said Majestic is budgeting more than a million dollars for it, and that doesn't include furnishings.''

Chase fingered the scar along his chin. ''Did he also tell you that, since the addition isn't part of the renovation, he'll be expected to fund a portion of it since he's one of the owners?''

''No. But since Majestic and he both own the hotel, that makes sense. He probably assumed I would realize as much.''

Or he hadn't bothered to worry about that little detail. The conference center hadn't been part of his plan to see Charbonnet destroyed. But the other man's greed to have Majestic help pay to construct the addition to his hotel would merely speed up Charbonnet's self-destruction. He should be happy about this, Chase told himself. It was what he wanted, what he had striven for when he had convinced Majestic to buy into the Saint Charles.

But the same sense of fairness that had compelled him to point out to Charbonnet the financial ramifications the addition would mean to him made Chase spell out those same warnings to Madeline now. Only it wasn't just a sense of justice, and he knew it. The realization annoyed him. He walked over and stood before her. "Do you think he's going to be able to come up with his share?" he asked, irritated with himself making his voice harder than he had intended.

Madeline's spine stiffened. "Well, if he couldn't, it would have been foolish for him to vote for the addition. Wouldn't it?"

Her defense of the other man only fueled his darkening mood. "You and I both know your father's very good at spending money, Princess. Particularly when it's other people's. You might want to remind him that this time he'll have to spend some of his own."

Her green eyes grew frosty. "Your company gave my father a lot of money for a share in his hotel, Chase. I suspect he'll use some of it."

"That is assuming he has any left." Given the other man's lavish life-style and penchant for entertaining, Chase suspected Charbonnet had gone through a considerable part of his proceeds from the sale. In truth, Chase had counted on him doing just that.

The heat of anger colored her cheeks and turned the green of her eyes to the shade of jade. "Whether he does or doesn't, I'd say my father's finances are none of your concern. Or mine, either, for that matter. I don't even know why we're having this conversation."

"Because the hotel *is* your concern." Chase drew in a long breath and released it. "I know how much you love this place, Madeline," he said, attempting to gentle his voice. "And I know how much you hated your father selling off a part of it and me coming here to run it."

"I'm over that, Chase. Really, I am. You've been good for the hotel." She averted her gaze. "I . . . I'm glad you're here."

He swallowed, taking comfort and pleasure in her admission. He tipped up her chin, forcing her to look at him. "But how will you feel if my firm ends up with an even larger share of your hotel?"

Madeline paled. She pushed his hand away and stood. "What do you mean?"

"I mean if your father fails to come up with his share of the money for the addition, and Majestic has to fund it, then Majestic will be forced to claim a larger interest in the hotel."

"Then don't do it. Forget about the conference center."

Chase shook his head. "Can't. Aside from the fact that your father and the board have already agreed to do it, the hotel needs the conference center if it's going to survive in the market here. The thing should have been added a long time ago. You know that yourself. That's the reason you tried to convince your father to build it before Majestic ever came on to the scene. And it's the reason I agreed to present your proposal to the board in the first place."

Her worried expression tore at him, made him feel guilty. "Listen, I'm not saying any of those things are going to happen. Maybe your father will prove me wrong and have no problem coming through with his share of the money when the time comes." He didn't think so. He had studied and tracked Charbonnet's spending habits for years and knew the other man didn't believe in putting money aside— not when there were parties to go to or things to buy. Still, he would give the other man the benefit of the doubt. Besides, he wanted to erase that sick look in Madeline's eyes. "I just want you to be prepared if he doesn't."

"Thanks. I appreciate it." The smile she gave him was overbright and as phony as the one she had worn at the reception announcing the hotel merger. "But I'm sure we're both worrying for nothing. The only reason my father sold an interest in the hotel in the first place was so he could save it. The place has needed repairs and renovations for a long time, and he simply couldn't do it on his own. He would never have agreed to the conference center addition if he didn't think he could come up with his share of the money. He would never do anything to risk losing the Saint Charles. It's the most important thing in the world to him."

And evidently it was more important than his daughter, Chase thought bitterly as Madeline politely thanked him once more and left. And it was one more reason for him to hate Henri Charbonnet and renew his vow to destroy him.

Returning to his desk, Chase sat down and buzzed through to Henri Charbonnet's office. "Sara, this is Chase McAllister. Is Mr. Charbonnet available?"

"I'm sorry, Mr. McAllister, he's not in his office right now."

"Has he gone for the day?"

"I believe he said he had an early dinner meeting," the secretary replied. "Would you like me to try to locate him for you?"

Silently Chase cursed the man and his never-ending social schedule. He'd lay odds the dinner meeting would take place in the hotel's dining room and be charged off as a business expense to the hotel as usual. "No. Just have him call me when he gets in tomorrow morning."

"Yes, sir."

"And, Sara, see what you can do to clear his calendar for a couple of hours. He and I need to go over a few things."

After hanging up the phone, Chase leaned back and rested his head against the soft expensive leather. Closing his eyes, he breathed deeply and caught a whiff of Madeline's perfume. Roses, he thought, disgusted to find himself becoming aroused by the lingering scent.

He opened his eyes and grabbed the contracts awaiting his approval from his In box. For the sake of his sanity, not to mention his body, he hoped his long-stemmed beauty didn't keep either one of them waiting much longer.

Seven

"You can? Oh, Kyle, you're a dream," Madeline said as she penciled in the name of the downtown hotel next to the last person on her list of overbookings. "I don't have to tell you how crazy it's been here with the Jazzfest going on. I really owe you for this one."

"Big-time," he assured her. "That's the fifth walk I've taken for you in the past two days."

And while she could throttle the new guy in reservations responsible for the overbookings that had forced her to scramble and call in favors to accommodate the displaced guests, she would not complain, Madeline told herself. The sellouts during the past two weekends would soon be a distant and bright memory when the dead summer months arrived. "I know. How about if I buy you lunch?"

"I'd prefer dinner. I haven't seen much of you lately, Madeline."

"I've really been busy, Kyle. They've started the renovations on the hotel, and there's the conference center addition that's about to get under way." Although neither were a part of her job, she wanted to be on hand as they polished and buffed her beloved hotel, restoring it to its original beauty. It was foolish. The hotel wasn't hers. It didn't even belong solely to her father anymore, but she still loved it.

"You doing okay?"

"I'm fine," she replied. If one could classify the constant butterflies in her stomach and lust in her heart every time she set eyes on Chase McAllister as "doing fine." Sighing, Madeline spun her chair around to look out the window of her office. She blinked, surprised to see the sunlight had already begun to slip away.

"So, how's it going with that McAllister fellow? You two still butting heads?"

"No. Things are better." At least where business was concerned, Madeline added silently. Her problems with Chase had little to do with the hotel. No, her problems centered on the fact that she wanted Chase. And each time he kissed her, each time he sent her one of those dark, hungry looks, she moved closer to succumbing to the temptation of going to bed with him. She didn't indulge in meaningless affairs for the sake of lust. That in itself should be reason enough not to become involved with him. But it wasn't the only reason she had held herself back. Fear of the aftermath of surrendering to that desire had been a big motivator. Because when he left in the fall, she was very much afraid Chase would take with him a piece of her heart.

"I'm glad to hear that. But you know if things don't work out, I mean if you were unhappy there, I could get you on here. The GM was interested when I mentioned you might be considering a change a couple of months ago. He said they're always looking for someone in the sales department who knows the hotel business."

"I appreciate that, Kyle. But sales isn't really where I want to be."

"Still hoping for a GM position, huh?"

"Yes. But I'm willing to settle for assistant GM and work my way up," she told him, smiling. Suddenly her smile froze as she sensed she was no longer alone. The hairs at the base of her neck lifted. Tiny fingers of awareness tiptoed down her spine. She knew even before turning around that she would find Chase.

"So, how about that dinner? We can discuss your plan for moving up the hotel ladder."

Easing her chair around slowly, her heart did a jig when she saw him standing in the doorway, his arms folded over his chest, that wicked smile on his face.

"Madeline?"

Madeline jerked her attention back to Kyle. "I'm sorry, Kyle. What did you say?"

The smile on Chase's mouth died at the mention of Kyle's name. His eyes narrowed, flickered menacingly as he watched her and listened. A thrill of pleasure shot through Madeline at the gleam of possessiveness in his look.

"I asked if you're free for dinner tonight."

"Dinner? Tonight?" Madeline repeated, knowing she sounded like an idiot and unable to do a thing about it with her heart hammering away.

"Madeline, is something wrong? You sound as though your brains turned to mush."

"No. I'm fine. Really," she insisted, tugging her eyes from Chase's face. Suddenly anxious, she asked, "Kyle, would you mind terribly if I took a rain check on that dinner? It's been a really long day for me and I'm a little tired."

"Sure. No problem. How about if I give you a call next week and set something up?"

"Yes. Next week will be fine. I'll wait to hear from you. Oh, and, Kyle, thanks again for helping out with the rooms. I really do appreciate it. You were a lifesaver."

"I thought I was a dream."

"That, too," Madeline managed in answer to his light-hearted response. After saying goodbye, she replaced the phone on its cradle.

Awareness hummed between them, and when she lifted her eyes to meet Chase's, her nerves sizzled under the intensity of his silent blue gaze. Then he was crossing the room, standing before her, pulling her to her feet and capturing her mouth with his.

From the fierceness of his expression Madeline had expected his kiss to be savage and hurried. But it was gentle and lingering instead. The unexpected sweetness of it was disarming and undermined any thought of her resisting.

He ran his tongue slowly along the shape of her lips, tempting her, teasing her with his heat. And when he whispered her name, it was *her* fingers sliding up his chest. *Her* fingers tangling in his hair. *Her* body on fire as he pulled her closer and deepened the kiss. Her ears rang. Her pulse beat so wildly she thought it would burst. She couldn't think. She forgot all about breathing. When his hands slid down her spine, cupped her buttocks and pressed her to him, Chase groaned.

Dragging her mouth free, Madeline gasped for air while her traitorous body continued to cling to him. Her head swam with dizzying pleasure as his mouth moved to explore her jaw, the sensitive spot beneath her ear. Grappling for what remained of her fraying control, Madeline pressed her hands against his chest. "Chase," she cried out his name. "Chase, please."

"Please what, Madeline?" he murmured hoarsely as he nibbled his way to the lobe of her ear.

Her breath hitched when he shifted his attention to her neck. "Please, stop."

His fingers tightened on her shoulders. She felt his body shudder, his chest rise and fall as he drew in several deep breaths and struggled for control. Then he lifted his head, rested it against hers for long moments before dropping his hands and stepping back.

The silence stretched between them until Madeline thought she would splinter with the tension. "Did...did you want me for something?"

Chase's head snapped up. His eyes shimmered with banked desire. "Oh, I want you, all right," he said, that dangerous smile tugging at his lips.

Madeline flushed. "I meant did you want to see me about hotel business?"

"No." He prowled around her office and finally commandeered the corner of her desk. Madeline waited for Chase to explain. But he didn't, evidently too intent on studying the crystal paperweight he had plucked from her desk. He held the sphere up to the light.

The jealousy that had gripped him by the throat when he had stood there listening to that wistful note in her voice and realized who she was talking to refused to let him go. It was the reason he had kissed her, to prove to himself that *he* was the one she wanted. Her sweet, hungry response had given him the answer. Yet the monster still clawed at his gut. "You going to have dinner with pretty boy?" Chase asked, pleased he had managed to sound casual when he was feeling anything but.

"I don't know. Probably," Madeline replied, her brow knitting as though confused by the question. "I guess I should. I owe him a favor for taking some of our hotel overbookings."

"Then it's still just business between you and him."

"Of course it's just business between us," she said impatiently.

"That's good, Princess." He looked away from the paperweight and directly into her eyes, disturbed by the relief her response brought him. "Because I don't share."

"Share!" The word was a breathless hiss.

"That's right." He knew the remark would set her off. He didn't care. He liked all that fire cloaked in softness. And he wanted it. He wanted *her*. All for himself. "It's another one of those lessons I never learned. I never could buy into that business of sharing what I considered mine," he explained, enjoying the flush of anger that colored her cheeks. Her green eyes sparked with fury. That stubborn chin of hers tipped up, daring him to take a poke at it.

Sweet heaven, so much passion, so much spirit, he thought. His body tightened painfully as he wondered what it would be like to bury himself in the heated silk between her thighs.

Not that he was likely to find out anytime soon, Chase lamented. Judging from Madeline's expression, she would rather strangle him than make love to him at the moment. He smiled at the notion, which only seemed to infuriate her more.

"I'll have you know I do not find it the least bit amusing or flattering to be referred to as though I'm a...a...a piece of candy," she sputtered.

"Not candy. Roses," Chase said, amused.

"Nor do I like your implying that I—" She stopped, a wrinkle forming a tiny crease between her brows as she stared at him in confusion. "What do you mean roses?"

"That's how I think of you. It's how I've thought of you from the first moment I set eyes on you. That day when you walked into the press conference wearing your little red suit with that pouty mouth of yours painted to match, you reminded me of a long-stemmed rose." Chase laughed, embarrassed at how foolish he must sound. "Hell, you even managed to smell like roses. You still do." And every time he was in the same room with her, just her scent was enough to set his body off.

"How do you expect me to respond to a statement like that?" she asked, her voice filled with exasperation.

"I don't." Chase set down the paperweight and grinned. "Have you eaten dinner yet?"

"No. I—"

"Great. Then you can have dinner with me."

She arched her brow in that imperious manner of hers. "Gee, it's so nice of you to *ask*," she said, emphasizing the fact that he hadn't asked her at all.

Chase laughed. "All right, Princess. We'll do it your way. Have dinner with me and I promise to *ask* you nice and properly to come with me to the Jazzfest tomorrow."

She blinked. "*You're* going to the Jazzfest?"

"Don't sound so shocked. I've never been before, and I have it on good authority it's a 'not to be missed' experience. I've even managed to get a couple of tickets for one of the off-site performances for what I'm told is one of your favorite groups." He pulled the Neville Brothers tickets from his pocket and waved them in front of her face, then stuffed them back in his pocket before she could snatch them from him.

"How in the world did you get those? Those tickets sold out within hours after they went on sale."

"Piece of cake," he lied. He had scrambled like crazy to get those tickets after Chloe James had mentioned the local group of musicians were one of Madeline's favorites. An ad in the paper and an obscene amount of money had proved the key. "Have dinner with me, and I'll let you in on my trade secret."

Madeline paused.

Chase studied her face. A warm softness filled his chest as he watched her battle with herself. He knew she had reservations about getting involved with him—and rightfully so. She was a woman with deep-seated roots, who believed in love and commitment. He was a wanderer who believed in neither. But he wanted her. And because he knew she wanted him, too, he couldn't simply walk away. He didn't want her to walk away either.

He reached out and stroked his finger along her jaw and watched the sensual fire begin to flicker once more in her eyes. "It's only dinner, Princess," he said as he continued to caress her soft skin. "That is unless I can coax you into—"

"Don't you dare say it, McAllister." She brushed his hand away from her cheek and grabbed her purse from the drawer in her desk. She marched to the door and turned. "If you want to join me for dinner, then let's go. But don't say another word about...about that."

"Don't say another word about what?" Chase asked innocently as he followed her to the elevator banks.

She glared at him and punched the button for the elevator. "About coaxing me into bed."

"Bed? Who said anything about coaxing you into bed? I was talking about coaxing you into having dessert." The elevator door whooshed open and saved her from having to reply. She hurried inside to join several hotel guests. Chase smiled in greeting before moving to stand next to Madeline. Leaning closer, he whispered into her ear, "But I have to say, I like your suggestion much better. It's all right with me if you'd rather just skip dessert and go back to your place."

"Can the seduction techniques, McAllister," she said as they stepped out into the lobby. "I get nasty when I go too long without food. Lunch was only a salad and that was nearly eight hours ago."

She started towards the hotel dining room, but Chase caught her arm. "My offer of dinner was personal, Madeline. Not business. I know the food's good here, but I'd rather go somewhere else." He wanted her away from here. Away from the hotel, her father and thoughts of his plans for revenge. "Do you mind?"

"No. Not at all," she said, a hesitant smile curving her lips. "But could you give me a minute first to speak with André? One of the hotel's guests had a problem with a room service order this morning. They're a delightful couple who've booked twenty rooms and a bridal luncheon next month for their daughter's wedding," she explained as they made their way past the front desk. "I offered them a complimentary dinner in the hotel tonight to make up for it." She slanted a glance up at him. "I hope that's okay. I mean I don't know what Majestic's policy is on things like that."

"The same as most businesses. Keep the customer happy."

"Good," she said, smiling again. "It was a judgment call on my part, but the Reynoldses seemed most appreciative of the offer."

Chase frowned. "Placating unhappy guests isn't part of your job, Madeline. You shouldn't have to be making decisions on how to handle those problems in the first place."

The smile disappeared along with the warmth. "I realize I probably should have cleared it through you or my father first," she told him, her voice growing as rigid as her spine, as they continued in the direction of the hotel's dining room. "But I guess I'm still not used to the idea of having my decisions or my judgment questioned."

Chase stopped. Taking Madeline by her stiff shoulders, he turned her to face him. "No one's questioning your decisions or your judgment, Princess. From everything I've seen, they're both excellent. What I'm asking is why *you* were the one who had to make the decision to begin with."

"I always make the decisions on guest problems," she tossed back.

Chase sighed. "I know. And that's my point. It's not your job to make them. Your father's getting paid a hefty salary to be the GM of this hotel, but you're the one doing most of the work."

"That's not true," she said defensively, but Chase noted that she didn't meet his eyes. She shrugged free of his grip, and they continued their trek to the dining room. "Mr. Reynolds was very upset, and my father wasn't here. He had an appointment outside of the hotel," she added quickly. "So the front desk called me."

The truth was that even when Charbonnet was at the hotel—which wasn't often—most of the staff came to Madeline anyway. The man was a user, Chase surmised bitterly. He had used Chase's mother, feeding the naive Katie McAllister with dreams and then snatching them away. And because of him, his mother had abandoned both her dreams and her son. Chase swallowed hard, fighting back the ugly memory of finding his mother's body.

And now Charbonnet was using Madeline, his own daughter. He had shouldered her with the responsibility of the daily operations of the hotel, but without ever giving her the title and respect that came with it. For some reason, Charbonnet's injustice to Madeline only fueled his hatred for the man, made him more determined than ever to strip him of what he loved most—his hotel.

And how will Madeline feel when you destroy her father? the voice inside him taunted as they reached the dining room's entrance.

The arrival of the maître d' saved him from answering. "Madeline. Monsieur Chase. Will you be joining us for dinner tonight?" a beaming André asked. "Chef has a new trout dish on today's special that is excellent."

Chase smiled at the debonair gentleman, all proud and proper in his black dinner jacket and bow tie. A fixture of the hotel, the French-born André had started as a busboy for Madeline's grandfather and worked his way up. He had been parking cars and hauling bags when Chase's own mother had worked here. "Not tonight, André. Madeline and I thought we'd check out the competition."

"Don't give me that look," Madeline told André, her voice filled with affection. "From what I can see, you don't have room for us anyway."

"For you and Monsieur Chase, I would make room," André assured her.

Madeline squeezed his hand. "I'm sure you would, and we appreciate it. But right now I just want to check to see if Mr. and Mrs. Reynolds have been in yet. They're the couple I told you about this morning."

While Madeline chatted with the maître d', Chase stepped to the side and allowed his gaze to wander over the crowded dining room. White-gloved waiters scurried around the tables, refilling water glasses, clearing away serving dishes and silver. The place was packed, the room humming with the din of voices, the clink of china and crystal, Chase noted approvingly. A deep, raucous laugh followed by the call for "another bottle of champagne" drew Chase's attention to a center table where a party of six sat wining and dining on the hotel's finest food and drink.

Chase scowled as he recognized the party's host—Henri Charbonnet. Anger ripped through him at the sight. The man hadn't been in his office all day. Nor had he responded to any of the messages Chase had left for him, asking for and then demanding the proposals from the decorators for refurbishment of the hotel suites. At Henri's insistence, he had agreed to allow the other man to handle bidding out the job of supplying new drapes and furnishings for the rooms. With the renovation work more than half-completed, the fabrics and furniture would need to be selected soon in order to arrive in time for the rededication ceremony in the fall. *Probably a stupid move on my part,* Chase decided as his annoyance with Charbonnet turned to something darker.

"Listen, if you want to rescind the dinner invitation, it's not a problem," Madeline said, the defensive note returning to her voice.

Chase jerked his gaze to her, not realizing she had concluded her conversation with the maître d' and rejoined him.

"I mean, if you've changed your mind. Just say so and spare me the stone-faced looks."

"I'm sorry," Chase told her. He gave himself a mental shake and attempted to shake off the anger that had gripped him at seeing Henri. "And I haven't changed my mind. I *want* to have dinner with you." He attempted a smile.

"Could have fooled me. You looked like you were ready to strangle someone."

"It's nothing to do with you. Let's go."

He started to usher her away, but Madeline slid her gaze to the center of the room, traveling in the direction where his had been moments earlier. "It's my father."

"Yeah. Look's like he's having a little dinner party. But if you don't mind, I'd rather we didn't join them. Like I told you earlier," he said, trying to recapture the lightness they had enjoyed. "I don't like sharing you."

She arched one dark brow at the comment, then her lips twitched at the corners in a smile. "All right, McAllister. I guess I'll let you get away with that this time. But only because I'm starving."

"Then I'd better see what I can do to satisfy your hunger, Ms. Charbonnet."

Chase caught that cool look she fired at him that said she recognized the double entendre but had no intention of biting. Laughing, he said, "Let's go."

"McAllister! Madeline!" Chase heard Charbonnet call out their names, saw him rise from his seat and start toward them. Chase cursed his luck. He didn't want to talk to or even look at the man. All he wanted was to be with Madeline, to forget her name was Charbonnet and that he hated her father.

Madeline stopped and looked back to the dining room's entrance. "Chase, he's seen us. We have to at least go over and say hello. It would be rude not to, and my father would be hurt if we refused. Don't worry." She offered him a smile and her hand. "We don't have to join them for dinner. I promise."

"All right. But I intend to hold you to that promise. And later," he murmured as her father approached, "I'm going to see if I can't get you to make a few more."

"Henri," Chase said, nodding his head in greeting as the other man joined them.

"McAllister." Henri acknowledged him with a tip of his head, then frowned when he noted Madeline holding Chase's hand.

"Hello, Father." Madeline went to her father and kissed his cheek.

"Hi, Baby." Henri gave her a quick hug and set her away. "You'll never guess who I saw today," he said, his green eyes twinkling as he looked at his daughter.

"I'm sure I can't imagine."

"Bradley. He was asking about you."

"That's nice," she said noncommittally.

Who in the hell is Bradley? Chase wondered as he noted the strain work its way into her smile.

"The boy's done very well for himself in San Francisco," Henri continued. "But he says his heart's still here in New Orleans. I suspect you might have something to do with that, Baby."

"Father, please."

"Henri, did you know I've been trying to reach you all day?" Chase cut in, disliking the unknown Bradley already.

"Yes." Henri shifted his attention back to Chase. "That's what Sara told me when she reached me in my car this afternoon." He gave Chase a friendly pat on the back. "You know how it is, Son. All those meetings and luncheons a hotelier has to participate in to keep his hotel's name out there. It doesn't leave much time for sitting around in the office. But enough shoptalk. Business can wait until tomorrow. Have you eaten dinner yet?"

"Madeline and I were just going out to get something," Chase replied.

"Going out? Whatever for? We've got the best food in the city right here. You two come on over and join me and my friends for dinner."

"Thanks, but I've already made reservations," Chase lied.

Henri frowned. "Well at least come over for a minute and let me introduce you to my guests. There's someone special I'd like you to meet, McAllister."

After following Henri into the dining room, introductions were made around the table. Then Henri moved to stand beside his last guest—the cool blonde who had been seated to his right. "And this lovely creature is Ms. Lana Duvernay. Lana, this is Chase McAllister with Majestic Hotels. Chase, Lana Duvernay with Duvernay Designs."

"Ms. Duvernay." Chase shook hands with the woman, not missing the size of the emerald rock on her finger or the Rolex watch on her wrist. Ironic, Chase thought as he watched the other woman exchange greetings with Madeline. Lana Duvernay fit the image he had once thought to saddle Madeline with—attractive, expensive and as cold as a northern winter. Madeline had certainly proved him wrong. With her sweep of dark hair, soft silken skin and made-for-kissing mouth, she had turned out to be an unknowing seductress. Especially when she smiled and looked at him with those expressive green eyes, the way she was doing now.

"I'm looking forward to working with you, Mr. McAllister. And please, do call me Lana."

Chase dragged his gaze away from Madeline and tried to focus his attention on Lana Duvernay. "I'm sorry, Ms. Duvernay. Lana," he amended at her chiding look. "Did you say we would be working together?"

Henri laughed. "Of course, she did. Where's your head tonight, McAllister? I just finished telling you that Lana's firm is going to be the one handling the redecorating of the hotel's suites."

Madeline held her breath as she felt Chase tense, saw him slice a narrowed glance at her father. *What was wrong?* she wondered, not for the first time since they'd left her office. The man shifted moods with the speed of an Indy driver— going from seduction to leashed fury in the space of a heartbeat.

"I wasn't aware that any decision had been made on the decorating firm yet," Chase told her father evenly, but Madeline hadn't missed the rigid set of his jaw, or the darkening blue of his eyes. "In fact, that's the reason I was trying to reach you today, Henri. To go over the proposals."

"Those proposals are a waste of time. Take my word for it. Lana's the best in the city. Why, I used her myself to redecorate my own place a few months ago, and she did an excellent job."

"I'm sure she did," Chase said, and Madeline fought back a shiver at the danger in that soft tone of voice. "And I'm sure Lana will understand that I'll still need to look over her proposal before any final decision can be made or any contracts can be signed on behalf of the hotel."

"Actually, I didn't submit a formal proposal," Lana explained, favoring both her father and Chase with another smile. "I'm familiar with the hotel and Henri's tastes, so when he mentioned the project to me I simply tossed out a few suggestions on how I would go about redecorating some of the suites. Henri thought they were good."

"They were excellent suggestions," Henri assured Chase, his voice growing louder, his face flushed an angry red. "That's why I gave Lana the job."

The scar on Chase's chin stretched into a thin white line as his jaw tightened. Madeline could all but feel the anger vibrating in him. *A cougar!* The notion shot through Madeline's thoughts as she watched Chase. A golden cougar with deadly blue eyes. Suddenly her pulse sprinted, and Madeline reached over and placed her hand on Chase's arm. "And I'm sure Lana won't mind jotting some of those suggestions down for you in the form of a proposal," Madeline offered. "Will you, Lana?"

"No. I don't guess it would be any problem. Would Monday be soon enough?" she asked Chase.

Chase hesitated a moment, then said, "Monday will be fine."

Madeline breathed a small sigh of relief. "Well, we've kept you from your meal long enough. Chase and I had better be going, or we'll be late for our own dinner."

Her father didn't ask that they join him again, for which Madeline was grateful. After saying their goodbyes, she walked silently beside a somber Chase.

She preceded him through the massive wood-and-glass doors at the entrance of the hotel and stepped outside into the clear spring night. The moon sat high in the sky, as though suspended from invisible wires, a glowing yellow ball against a black canopy dusted with twinkling white lights. A breeze swept by, carrying with it the scent of gardenias from a neighboring bush. Madeline breathed in deeply as much to enjoy the sweet fragrance as to ease her nerves.

"*Are* we still going to dinner together?" Chase asked, coming to stand beside her.

The anger still clung to him, as did the tension. "We are, unless you've decided to renege on your invitation." From the distant expression on his face, she half expected him to do just that.

"I haven't."

Along with the clip in his voice, there was resignation and pride in his eyes that told her he expected her rejection and was prepared for it. The defensive response cried out to her of loneliness, reminding her that despite his confident manner, Chase had spent his childhood faced with rejection. The realization yanked painfully at her heart. "Neither have I," she told him, calling herself a fool even as she uttered the words. She was falling hard for him, Madeline admitted. She would be crazy not to get out before she fell any harder.

Evidently she was crazy, Madeline decided. She smiled up at him. "At least, not before I find out how you got those tickets to the Neville Brothers."

Some of the stiffness seemed to go out of him at her teasing remark. His mouth curved at the corners. "Then it's liable to be a long night, because I don't give up trade secrets easily."

"Then I guess I'll have to see what I can do to loosen your tongue."

She still hadn't managed to loosen his tongue three hours later when Chase walked her to her front door—at least not about how he had gotten the tickets. The little café he had taken her to had been off the beaten path and a far cry from the elegant dining at the Saint Charles. But the shrimp and pasta dish they had decided on and the wine Chase had selected had been delicious. And so was Chase's company.

She had managed to discover that Chloe had been his source of information that the Neville Brothers were among her favorite groups. She had also discovered that they shared a love of theater musicals, action films and jazz, but would never agree on politics or the fact that anything with chocolate in it would simply have to be the better dessert. They had discussed a dozen things, but not a word about the earlier scene with her father. Though the scene and its repercussions worried her, Madeline was loath to mention it for fear of spoiling the evening.

"I had a lovely time tonight," she told him when they reached the alcove at her door.

"It doesn't have to end yet." He traced the line of her jaw with his thumb.

She found the texture of his rough skin against her softness strangely erotic, and it sent tiny arrows of warmth flowing through her. "I think it might be better if it did."

Giving her that wicked smile, he moved in, slipping his arms around her waist and pulling her against him. Slowly, gently, he brushed his mouth against hers. "Better for whom?" he whispered, lifting his head a fraction.

Moonlight shunted across his face, and there was no mistaking the desire in his eyes. An answering desire shuddered through her. "For me," she finally managed to say, pulling herself back from the precipice.

"Madeline." Chase started to kiss her again.

"No." She pressed her fingers to his lips. She squeezed her eyes shut as she struggled for control. If he kissed her again, she wouldn't have the will to resist him.

Chase nipped her fingers with his teeth. Madeline's eyes opened instantly, and she tried to pull away. Chase caught her wrist, keeping her fingers pressed against his mouth while he alternately nipped and kissed them, then laved them with his tongue.

A shiver went through Madeline, sending sweet warmth through her body, between her thighs. "You're a dangerous man, Chase McAllister."

"There's nothing wrong with a little danger. Especially if it's what we both want."

"Maybe," Madeline told him as she managed to extricate her hand and tried to slow the hammering of her pulse. "But I have to be sure it's what *I* want. I...I need more time, Chase. I have to think of the repercussions."

"What repercussions?"

"There's my job at the hotel for one thing. And then there's the problem between you and my father. I don't know how either of those things would be affected if we became lovers."

Chase caught her chin and tipped it up, forcing her to look at him. Hunger, hot and demanding, burned like flames in his blue eyes. "It's not a question of 'if' we become lovers, Madeline. It's only a question of 'when.' And make no mistake about it, when I do make love with you, it won't have a damn thing to do with the hotel or your father. And it'll have everything to do with this."

He took her mouth then. Plundering, ravaging, wringing from her a response every bit as greedy and consuming as his. When he tore his mouth free, Madeline leaned her head back against the door.

"Go ahead and do your thinking, Madeline," he said.

She was too fascinated by the way his chest heaved beneath his shirt as he sucked in air to tell him she couldn't think at all right now. She wasn't even sure she could breathe.

"Sooner or later you're going to see that I'm right. And then we can take that next step." He brushed his thumb across her bottom lip, and the heat started to flow inside of her again. "It's going to be very good between us," he whispered. "For both our sakes, don't make us wait too much longer."

Eight

"**H**ow about something to drink?" Chased asked Madeline as they milled around the fairgrounds with the thousands of others who had turned out for the Jazzfest. A horse racing track for most of the year, the grounds had been converted for the annual festival that served as a showcase for the city's musical talents. Many of those performers who had gone on to fame and fortune made their way back each spring for the event.

"Sure. I thought I saw a lemonade stand somewhere over there." Madeline shoved her sunglasses up on top of her head. Squinting against the bright sunlight, she scanned over in the direction where a myriad of food booths had been set up for the festival. Mild temperatures and sunshine had brought out a record number of music lovers for the last weekend of the festivities. People, young and old, crowded around the rows of booths that served up cold drinks, liquor and a host of the spicy local dishes.

"I think it might have been all the way over at the other end," Madeline said, indicating the opposite side of the long stretch of stands.

"Then let's go see if we can find it."

She looked younger and more carefree today, Chase thought, enjoying the rear view Madeline provided as she led them past the mouth-watering scents of gumbos, *étouffées* and numerous Creole delicacies. Probably something to do with the navy-checked walking shorts, crisp white blouse and flat shoes she was wearing. Chase smiled. He had half expected to see her in another one of her suits when he had picked her up that morning.

"Look, there it is," Madeline said, turning to him even as she pointed out the refreshment booth near the end of the concession stands. She stopped. "What?"

He shifted his attention to her face. "Hmmm?"

"What are you smiling about?"

"You."

Madeline's eyes narrowed suspiciously. "And exactly what is it about me that's put that devil's smile on your face?"

"Devil's smile?"

"Yes. Devil's smile," she told him as they continued in the direction of the lemonade booth. "Don't play the innocent with me, Chase McAllister. You have a wicked smile and you know it. I've certainly seen you use it often enough to make some poor female's pulse twitter."

"And what about you, Madeline?" he asked, giving her the devil's smile she had accused him of using. "Does my smile make your pulse twitter?"

She shot him that duchess-to-peasant look and tipped up her chin. "If it does, I'm not about to tell you. That ego of yours doesn't need any more stroking. It's already oversize. So quit fishing for compliments, McAllister, and tell me what it is about me that's put that wicked smile on your face."

"Oh, there're quite a few things about you that can bring a smile to my face, Princess. So far, most of them have been fantasies." And those fantasies had required quite a number of long, cold showers.

"McAllister." His name was a warning growl.

"All right," Chase said, laughing. "It's the outfit."

Madeline stopped again. "My outfit?"

"Yeah, those little checkered shorts and top thing you're wearing."

She looked down at the clothes she was wearing and back up at him. "What's wrong with what I have on?"

"Not a thing," he said, allowing the smile to spread across his face. "I like your suits. I really do. I even like those ridiculous colored heels you wear to match them. But there's something to be said for the sight of you in shorts, Ms. Charbonnet." He slid his gaze down the length of her legs and back up again. "You make quite an enticing picture."

"Is that so?"

"Most definitely," he assured her.

She arched her brow imperiously, then subjected his shorts, polo shirt and bare legs to a slow assessment similar to the one he had just given her. "Well, the same can be said for you, Mr. McAllister." She circled him, evidently extending her appraisal of him to include all angles. When she completed the circle and faced him once again, she quipped, "Especially the view from the rear."

Chase threw back his head and laughed. "Come on. Let's go get that lemonade."

Ten minutes later he had successfully managed to make it to the front of the line and secured two lemonades. Turning to Madeline, he stole a quick kiss before handing her the cup. "So, who's Bradley?" he asked idly as they made their way back to the performance area.

She slanted him a puzzled look that told him she thought the change of subject and the question came out of left field.

It probably had. The question had skittered through his thoughts when Henri had mentioned the name yesterday and Madeline's usually open expression had closed up. For a moment it had triggered an uneasy feeling inside him.

Then he had become too caught up in his anger with Henri to think of it further. But last night, when Madeline had once again denied them both the consummation of the passion that throbbed between them, the question had come back to nag at him.

"What makes you ask?" She licked a drop of lemonade from her lower lip.

Chase beat back the unexpected rush of desire to replace her tongue with his own. "Just curious," he finally said. He took a long, cooling drink from his own cup. "You got a funny look on your face when your father mentioned his name yesterday. I got the impression that maybe there was something between you and this Bradley character."

"Eastman. His name is Bradley Austin Eastman. His family owns a small chain of hotels called the Eastman Arms."

"I've heard of it," Chase muttered. With four luxury hotels located on the West Coast and one in New Orleans, the Eastman Arms was essentially a competitor of Majestic Hotels, albeit on a smaller scale. While it didn't surprise him that the son of an old-line hotel family would be of interest to Madeline, it did irritate the hell out of him. "So, *is* there something going on between you and this Eastman guy?"

"There was at one time. *Was* being the operative word. We were engaged for a while."

Engaged. Something savage and angry slammed in his chest at the wistful look in her eyes. Her words rang in his ears, setting off possessive instincts he didn't realize he even had. Chase threw his lemonade cup into a trash barrel and shoved his hands into his pockets to stop himself from reaching for her and forcing her to admit she was his. "You still hung up on him?" he asked, unable to keep the hardness out of his voice. "Is that the reason you've been tying yourself up in frustrated little knots over whether or not to go to bed with me? Because you've still got a thing for this Eastman guy?"

Her green eyes sparked. Madeline looked down at the cup of lemonade she was holding in her hand and back up at him.

"I wouldn't if I were you," he warned. "You may not care for my method of retaliation. And I promise, I would retaliate, Princess."

Chase watched her battle with the impulse to toss the drink in his face. With a sound of disgust, she opted for dumping it into the trash barrel instead. "No, I am not 'hung up' on Bradley. Nor am I tied up in 'frustrated little knots' over whether or not to go to bed with you," she said, mimicking his tone. "But if frustrated's how *you're* feeling, then maybe you should find someone who shares your high opinion of yourself and hop into bed with *her.*"

Chase caught her arm to stop her from flouncing off. "I don't want someone else, Madeline. I want you."

"Then you have a problem. Because I'm not sure I want to take part in a . . . a quick weekend fling. No matter how memorable it might prove to be."

"You're right about one thing. When we do go to bed together, it will be memorable. For both of us. But it won't be quick, Madeline. You can bet on that. And it's going to take a hell of a lot more than a weekend to satisfy either one of us."

Color crawled up her cheeks. Her gaze swept the area around them. "Is that supposed to convince me?" she asked, lowering her voice, but not the heat behind her words.

"No. Just stating the facts."

Madeline made a strangled sound. "I've had enough of the verbal volleying. I'm leaving. I never should have come in the first place."

"Madeline, wait," he called out, staying her movements. Chase sighed, the anger going out of him as he realized how out of line he had been. For a man who never allowed his libido or a woman to tie him up in knots, both his desire for Madeline Charbonnet and the woman herself were doing a great job of doing just that. "I'm sorry. I've been acting like a jackass."

"You won't get any argument out of me on that."

He managed not to flinch at the bite in her voice. "My only excuse is that I want you so badly I can't think straight. I don't think I've been in this state of constant sexual frustration since I was a raw teenager. And even then, I'm not sure it was *this* bad." He raked his hand through his hair. "I'm sorry. I had no right to come at you the way I did about Eastman."

"No you didn't."

Chase frowned. That last had grated. Mostly because he knew it was true. He had no claims on Madeline. None whatsoever. "I guess you'll just have to chalk it up along with my ego on that scorecard of faults that you're keeping on me. I'm feeling a bit territorial where you're concerned, Princess. I'm not particularly happy about that, but there it is. And while you're condemning me, you might as well know the thought of you with Eastman makes me want to knock his head off."

"That's some apology, McAllister."

Chase shrugged. "It's the best I can manage. I'm seldom sorry for my actions or my words. As far as my feelings, they're my own. And I won't apologize for them." He had apologized because he had owed her as much. If it wasn't good enough, then so be it. He wouldn't beg for her forgiveness or anyone's. "If you're expecting me to grovel, then you're out of luck."

"No. I can see you're not the groveling type. Probably a testosterone thing." The storm clouds in her eyes moments earlier gave way to something softer, lighter. Her lips curved with a hint of a smile. "But then, I have to admit, you do have a way of boosting a woman's ego. Poor Bradley. Imagine getting decked for simply being engaged to me once."

Chase scowled. He didn't feel the least bit sorry for poor Bradley. "Do you still want to leave?" Chase asked, not quite sure how to gauge Madeline's response.

"Not unless you're lying about having tickets for the Neville Brothers show and we need to try hustling some up outside of the club."

The knot that had twisted like a pretzel in his stomach loosened. "They're not fake. They'll get us in."

"Then why don't we enjoy the rest of the day like we planned." Madeline curled her fingers around his. "Ever done any Cajun dancing?"

"No. But I think I'll settle for just listening to the music."

"No one just *listens* to Cajun music. You have to feel it. Come on." She tugged on his hand and started toward the performance area. "I'll teach you."

Laughing, Madeline dropped down to rest on the table throw she had spread out under one of the oak trees. She drew a deep breath. "Whew! It's been ages since I've done any Cajun dancing. I forgot how exhausting it can be."

"Now she tells me," Chase grumbled as he lowered himself beside her. He held his hand to his side. "I hope you're not intent on doing anything more than listening to the music for the rest of the afternoon. Because if you are; I should warn you I'll be lucky if I have enough energy left to make it back to the car, let alone drive to the Quarter for that show tonight."

Madeline laughed. "It wasn't *that* bad."

"Speak for yourself, Ms. Cajun dance queen. My calf muscles may never forgive me." Groaning, he rubbed the muscles in his leg.

"Oh, stop all the bellyaching, McAllister." She pushed his hands out of the way. Replacing them with her own, she began kneading the muscles in his legs. "You were having a great time. Admit it."

"All right, it was fun." Closing his eyes, Chase moaned as she worked her fingers over the tight muscles.

"You looked good out there, too. A natural." She used her thumbs to massage the hard flesh.

"You made me look good."

Madeline grinned. "You did that yourself." She looked up from his leg to the open collar of his green shirt, where she could just make out the dusting of more dark blond hair. The tan on his legs, arms and neck extended in a wash of warm gold over his strong jawline and high cheekbones. His face was tipped up, exposing the jagged scar on his chin to the sunlight that filtered through the trees. His eyes were closed, protecting her from their silvery blue heat.

"Maybe, but you looked even better. Ah, that feels good," he said, his lips curving in a sensuous smile. Pleasure, stark and powerful, spread over his face.

Madeline's pulse sped up as she wondered how Chase looked after he had made love. Chiding herself for the dangerous direction of her thoughts, she tore her gaze free and went back to work on his calf muscles. The man was far too sexy for his own good, Madeline decided, still feeling the effects of that smile. And he was dangerous to her peace of mind.

"I'm beginning to suspect that blue blood of yours isn't so pure after all," Chase told her. He eased his eyes open to lazy half slits. "Are you sure you don't have some Cajun ancestors you've never mentioned?"

"Not that I know of," she replied, her heartbeat quickening at the warmth in his eyes as he watched her. Uncomfortable under his scrutiny, Madeline shifted her ministrations to his other leg. "What about you? Mississippi's not too far away," she commented, trying to keep her voice light. She remembered him mentioning that he and his mother had moved to New Orleans when he was still an infant. "Any Cajuns in your family tree?"

The smile dissolved in his eyes first, and then on his lips. "I don't have any idea. I know the name McAllister is Scottish, and my mother was part Irish. But that's about all I know."

"No grandparents? Or cousins?"

Chase shook his head. "I don't have any other relatives that I know of. My mother told me that my father died before I was born. That might or might not be true. But I suspect that even if he is dead, they were probably never really married."

Madeline's fingers stilled on his legs. "Why would you think that?"

He shrugged. "Little things mostly. There were never any pictures of my father around the house when I was growing up. No photos or scrapbooks or wedding pictures."

"Maybe they just couldn't afford them."

"Maybe. But there were other things. She never spoke of any family—hers or my father's."

"She could have been estranged from your father's family and hers, too," Madeline offered.

"That's what I used to tell myself, too. Or maybe *hoped* was more like it. The first year or two that I was at St. Mark's I used to pretend that I did have grandparents, that there had been a big falling out between them and my mother, that they didn't even know I existed. And then when they found out that they had a grandson, they would be excited and happy. They would come to the home for me and take me away to live with them."

Madeline swallowed past the lump in her throat as she envisioned a sad, lonely young Chase. So hungry for love, for a family. She had not realized just how blessed she had been growing up—to have both of her parents and her grandparents, to have known their love, to still have her father with her. How awful for Chase, she thought, not to have that sense of belonging, that security of knowing you are loved. "Did you ever try to find them? Your grandparents, I mean."

"No."

Suddenly she wanted him to have those things, that sense of being a part of a family, of knowing who he was. Maybe it wasn't too late. "Why not? Chase, you could have family you don't even know about. Cousins, or aunts and uncles, or grandparents who don't even know you exist."

"I don't."

"You can't know that. Not if you haven't tried to find out." The idea seemed to catch fire inside her. "Your being here in New Orleans again it's...it's like an omen. Why don't you try to find out. I'll help you.''

"No."

"But why not?"

"Because there isn't anyone," he told her.

"But how can you be sure if you haven't even tried?" Madeline insisted.

He looked at her then, his silver eyes cold and far older than his years. "Because the State already tried. Believe me, the social welfare departments weren't any more anxious to take another kid into the system back then than they are now. There have always been too many unwanted kids declared wards of the State. After my mother died they tried to locate some family member to take me."

Madeline's hopes plummeted. "And they didn't find anyone?"

His lips thinned. "They came up with the guy they thought was my grandfather. My mother had named him as a secondary beneficiary on an insurance policy and listed his relationship as her father. They let him know that my mother was dead and that I had been placed in St. Mark's.''

"What happened?" Madeline asked, but from the expression on his face, she suspected she already knew the answer.

"He claimed he didn't have a daughter anymore. Said his daughter had died more than eight years ago, and he had no grandchildren."

Madeline moved over to him and clasped his hand. "Chase, I'm sorry."

"Don't be," he told her, squeezing her fingers lightly. "It was a long time ago. That old man meant nothing to me. His not wanting me didn't change the fact that I know my mother loved me and wanted me. That's enough for me. Did I tell you she's the reason I went into the hotel business to begin with?"

"Yes, you did," Madeline replied, pleased to see some of the coldness leave his eyes.

"She loved the old hotels, claimed that they had character and ghosts."

"Ghosts?"

"Yes," Chase said. A smile tugged at the corners of his lips. "She claimed that the ghosts of those people who stayed in the hotel's rooms came back to replay the happy times they spent there."

"Only happy ghosts inhabit a hotel?" Madeline asked, intrigued and touched by the concept. She moved to sit beside Chase.

Chase chuckled. "Probably the unhappy ones, too. But my mother didn't believe anyone who stayed in a grand hotel could be unhappy."

"She sounds like a very special woman."

"She was. You would have liked her."

Madeline leaned her head on his shoulder. "I'm sure I would have. I heard what you told Ruthie about her waiting tables to support you. That couldn't have been easy."

"It wasn't. But she never complained. Not once. Not even during those last few weeks when she must have been feeling so miserable."

"Was . . . was she ill for a long time before she died?"

Chase remained silent so long Madeline thought he hadn't heard her.

"My mother didn't die from any disease, Madeline. Not unless you call getting dumped by her married lover a disease."

There was an anger, a hatred in his tone that sent shivers down Madeline's spine. She drew away slightly to study his face. His eyes were as cold and hard as his voice, making her even more uneasy.

"She committed suicide when the guy she was in love with broke things off to go back to his family."

And in doing so, she had left her only son to face the world all alone. Madeline placed her head against his chest, wrapped her arms around him, wanting to offer comfort for the boy he had been, for the man he now was.

"I'm sorry." The words seemed so inadequate, but they were the only ones she could think of. "I can't even begin to imagine what that must have been like for you. I'm not sure I could have handled it."

"You would have. You're a lot stronger than you think, Princess." His fingers moved up and down the line of her spine.

She smiled into his shirt and found her heart losing more ground. She had been able to resist him when her attraction to him had been merely physical. But the pull to him was no longer only a physical one. How could it be when the more time she spent with him, the more she learned about him, the more deeply her feelings for him became engaged. "You've done so much with your life," she told him, thinking of all he had been through as a child, all he had had to overcome. "You've managed to carve out a successful career for yourself. And it's obvious from the things you've said about your mother that you don't blame her...hold her weakness against her."

Chase's hand stilled on her back. "I've never blamed my mother for taking her life. Not ever," he said, his voice losing the warmth that had been there only moments ago. "The only person I blame is the man who used her, who made her fall in love with him and then tossed her and her feelings aside when he grew tired of her. He's the one I blame for her death. He's the one I hate."

The bitterness behind the words sent a shudder of uneasiness down Madeline's spine. Long moments passed in silence, and she sensed the struggle in Chase. She wanted to ask him what he meant, if he knew who the man was who had caused his mother to take her life.

But before she could find the words or the courage, Chase was easing her away from him. "Enough about the past. I'd much rather dwell on the present," he told her, effectively ending the subject. He flashed her a wicked grin. "Ready to go back to your apartment and make wild, passionate love with me?"

Relieved that the darkness in him had passed, Madeline followed his lead and let go of the heavy moment. She shot him a quelling glance.

"That's what I was afraid of," Chase told her with a deep sigh as he urged her to her feet. "If I'm not going to get to explore that gorgeous body of yours, then I might as well let you show me the rest of the Jazzfest."

"Be glad to." Madeline shook out the tablecloth. With Chase's help she folded it and stuffed it inside her shoulder bag. "There's a couple of country-and-western groups if you want to take a stab at line dancing. Or we could check out the jazz. Any preferences?"

"Depends."

"On what?" Madeline asked as Chase took the bag from her and slung it over his own shoulder.

Linking his fingers with hers, Chase tugged her to him and kissed her slowly, tenderly. When he lifted his head, he whispered, "On which one will make you more susceptible to my charms."

"I'm already too susceptible to your charms." She took a step back.

"Really?" He gave her the knee-weakening smile again as they meandered back toward the performance area. "Want to go back to your place, after all?"

"I said I was susceptible, McAllister. Not over-whelmed," she returned, unable to keep the smile out of her voice. "You might want to try slowing down that libido of yours."

"I've got a better idea," Chase told her. He stopped and gave her another kiss—this one deeper, lingering and much more tempting. "Why don't you try to catch up."

Nine

Could a man die from sexual frustration? Chase wondered idly, as he tossed his pencil down on the proposals he had been studying and waited for Madeline to return his call. If so, chances were he would be dead by the time Madeline did catch up to him. Sighing, he yanked his tie loose and leaned back against the chair at his desk. The rest of their day at the Jazzfest and the concert that evening had been magical. In truth, he couldn't remember a date that he had enjoyed more or one he had found more fulfilling—at least on an intellectual level. Madeline was bright, funny and easy to talk to.

She was also sexy as hell. Her response to his stolen kisses had made his body tremble and his loins ache. Desire had hummed between them like a living flame. And when he had taken her home and pulled her into his arms that night, he had wanted nothing more than to be consumed by that heat—by Madeline's heat.

Stifling a groan, Chase squeezed his eyes shut as memory

sent him spinning back...back to that night, back to the feel of Madeline in his arms....

"I want you," he murmured against her neck. The scent of roses on her skin tempted him, and his mouth inched its way to the base of her throat to the open collar of her blouse. Her breasts arched against the fabric, rising and falling in rapid succession as her breathing quickened. Chase flicked open one button and then another, gaining access to the swell of her breasts. Lowering his head, he ran his tongue across the soft sweet skin.

Madeline shuddered, sending another stab of desire through him with her response. Quickly he flicked open the next two buttons and released the clasp at the front of her bra. He brushed aside the piece of lace. "God, you're beautiful," he told her, cupping her breasts with his hands. He stroked the nipples with his thumbs, and another shudder went through her. Unable to resist, he lowered his head and covered one nipple with his mouth.

"Chase."

His name was a strangled cry on her lips that sent another shiver of need through him. Excited, hungry for more of her, he shifted his mouth to minister to her other breast. He heard her breath hitch as his tongue swirled around the aureole. When he took the rose-hued tip into his mouth, Madeline cried out his name again.

Chase pulled her blouse free from the waistband of her shorts. Barely aware of the nails biting into his shoulders, slowly he opened the remaining buttons one by one, tasting each inch of skin unveiled to his mouth. Releasing the button of her shorts, he dropped to his knees. He slid his tongue into her navel, then gently nipped the soft flesh of her abdomen as he worked his way to the lace edge of her panties.

Madeline gasped. "Chase, please." She urged him to his feet. Her eyes were wild untamed flames of green as she pulled his mouth to hers.

Groaning, Chase pressed her body against the wall. Need ripped through him as he devoured her mouth, his tongue tangling and mating with hers. He claimed her breasts with his hands, kneading, squeezing the mounds of feminine flesh. He lifted his head, angled his mouth, then moved in, kissing her again. Easing his hand down her rib cage, he spread his fingers over her stomach, past the gaping zipper and inside the thin silk of her panties. He cupped her femininity, then slipped a finger inside her sweet warmth. She was wet and hot and ready for him. The realization nearly sent him over the edge. Chase tore his mouth free to watch her face as he stroked the sensitive nub at her center, slowly inserting his finger into her and drawing out almost completely before entering her again. Her head moved from side to side. Her fingers clung to him.

He felt the first shudder rush through her, and an answering tide of satisfaction swept through him. "Look at me, Madeline," he commanded, needing to see the desire in her eyes and know it was for him.

Her eyelashes fluttered, and she looked at him out of eyes glazed over with passion and pleasure. The ache in his loins grew even more painful at the raw desire he saw there. His fingers increased their rhythm, and when another spasm ripped through her body, Chase held on to her. "Don't fight it, Madeline. Take it. Ride it," he said. When she reached the crest and cried out, Chase caught her mouth and swallowed her protests as she rode out the storm.

Madeline pulled her mouth free. The air was thick with the scent of passion and the sound of their breathing. In the dim light of her foyer, her lips looked ripe and swollen from his kisses, her cheeks flushed from the pleasure he had given her. The eyes that stared back at him were wide, luminous and filled with desire.

Her hands trembled as she reached up to touch his face. Chase kissed the fingertips that traced his mouth and forced himself to remain still as she moved to the jagged scar along his chin down to the vee of his shirt. Chase's breath caught in his throat as she continued her exploration, traveling down his rib cage and stomach to the waistband of his pants.

When she hesitated at his belt buckle, Chase thought he would go mad. "Touch me, Madeline," he pleaded, his

voice strained with need. He pressed her hand against him.
"Feel how much I want you."

She stroked his hardness, and Chase bit back a moan. He
squeezed his eyes shut as she eased down his zipper and
slipped her hand beneath his briefs. When her fingers closed
around his throbbing shaft, Chase groaned. *Sweet heaven,
he wanted her. Couldn't ever remember wanting anyone
more.*

He opened his eyes to find her watching him. Her green
eyes were wide with what looked like surprise and innocence. It was the innocence that threw him, even as it excited him. Chase wondered how someone so sensuous could
not recognize the power of her own sensuality. But when she
stroked his length, he forgot about thinking. All he could do
was feel . . . and want.

Chase kissed her again. He thrust his tongue between her
lips, mating her mouth to his. His body shuddered as their
tongues danced in anticipation of the sweet heat that
awaited the joining of their bodies.

She stroked him again, and Chase jerked his mouth free.
Before he could warn her how close he was to cheating them
both, she brushed the tip of his manhood with her thumb.
Chase sucked in his breath. She repeated the movement, and
he captured her hand as need sliced through him with the
sharpness of a razor's edge. He pressed her fingers against
his chest. "Where's your bedroom?" he growled, his voice
dark and husky with desire.

Madeline's head jerked up at his question. Her body went
rigid. "Chase, I didn't mean— That is, I—"

Chase's stomach clenched, her words striking him in the
gut like a fist. His body screamed at her denial.

"I never meant for this to happen. I told you I needed
time..."

Chase bit off a curse. He gritted his teeth as her retreat
echoed in his ears. She wanted him as much as he wanted
her, and once more she was going to deny them both. Chase
looked at her mouth and fought the urge to take those lips
again, to kiss her, to touch her and ignite the passion until

she had no choice but to surrender to the desire throbbing between them.

Pride, stubborn and simple, held him back. He wanted Madeline. But he wanted her to make the decision for them to become lovers with her eyes open, because it was what she wanted, not because she had been coerced with promises of love or in the heat of the moment.

"Chase, I'm sorry. I didn't mean..." She paused and finished straightening her clothes. "I didn't intend for things to get so out of hand."

"How long are you going to make us wait, Madeline?" he asked, unable to keep the frustration out of his voice.

Her chin angled up, even as color flooded her cheeks. "Despite my actions tonight, I'm not a tease, Chase. And I swear I'm not playing games with you."

"Don't you think I know that?"

"Then why are you so angry with me?" she demanded.

"I'm not angry with you. I'm angry with myself."

"Why?" she asked, her expression puzzled.

"Because you're still not ready for an affair with me, and I've been ready since the moment I laid eyes on you three months ago." Chase dragged his hands through his hair. He let out his breath. "And because I'm doing a lousy job of keeping my promise to let you catch up with me."

"I might not ever catch up."

"You will," he told her, confident that it was only a matter of time.

But that had been more than a week ago. And judging by the way Madeline had avoided him since that night, he was no longer quite so sure.

"Where is he?"

Chase jerked his thoughts back to the present at the sound of Henri Charbonnet's voice.

"You mean Chase? I mean, Mr. McAllister?" Ellen, his secretary asked.

"Of course I mean McAllister."

"He's in his office," Ellen informed Charbonnet. "I'll buzz through and tell him you're here to see him."

"Don't bother. I'll tell him myself." Charbonnet shoved the door open and stormed into Chase's office, clutching a crumpled sheet of hotel stationery in his fist.

"Something I can do for you, Henri?" Chase offered calmly, taking in the mottled color of the other man's face.

"Yes," he snarled. "You can start remembering just *who* it is that owns this hotel."

"If memory serves me correctly, it's owned by Majestic Hotels and you," Chase returned.

"That's right. *I* own this hotel. Not you." Charbonnet's nostrils flared. "So who the hell do you think you are, sending this—this letter to Lana Duvernay?" He threw the mangled sheet of paper down on Chase's desk.

Steepling his fingers, Chase gave a cursory glance to the letter he had sent to the decorator, thanking her for her efforts and informing her he had chosen another firm whose prices were more in line with their budget. He looked up again at Charbonnet. "*I'm* the person who's responsible for seeing that the renovation of this hotel comes in on budget—something it won't do if I use your friend Lana Duvernay to redecorate the suites. I've chosen another firm to do the work."

"You can't do that. I've already promised Lana the job."

"Then you'll just have to break that promise, because we're not using her firm. Her prices were out of line—something you would have known if you'd bothered to look at the other proposals we received. She was the highest of the three firms who bid for the job. Take a look and see for yourself." He picked up the proposals and tossed them on the corner of the desk in front of Charbonnet. "Everything she's proposed—the wall coverings, the drapes, even the carpet—it's way over budget and thirty percent higher than the other bids."

Charbonnet didn't so much as even glance at the other offers. "Of course Lana's prices were higher. She's the best. If you want the best, you have to pay for it."

"But *you're* not the one paying for it," Chase reminded him. "Majestic Hotels is."

Henri's face flushed a deeper shade of red. He leaned forward, fury in his eyes. "Listen, you bastard, this is still my hotel. *I'm* its executive director and *I'm* the one who calls the shots around here. Not you. And *I* say Lana Duvernay gets the job."

Chase came to his feet, barely able to contain the anger and hatred gnashing around inside him. Placing his palms flat on the desk, he leaned closer and looked into Henri's eyes. "No, Charbonnet. You listen," he said, his voice hard and deadly, matching the feelings the other man elicited in him. "You may hold the title of executive director of this hotel, but it and the people who work here are no longer a part of your private little empire to command as you please. You're not the one calling the shots now. You gave up that right when you sold controlling interest to Majestic Hotels. And like it or not, *I'm* the one who calls the shots for Majestic. And I say your pal Lana Duvernay *does not* get the job."

"We'll just see about that. You've overstepped your bounds on this one, McAllister. You forget you're nothing but a flunky for Majestic, but I intend to see that you're reminded of that fact." He straightened, moving a few steps away before turning back to face Chase.

"Is that so?"

"Yes. And once I've talked to your superiors at Majestic, we'll see just which one of us will be calling the shots."

"Why don't we find out right now?" Chase shoved the phone toward Charbonnet. "Go ahead. Make the call."

Chase waited, but when the other man made no move toward the phone, Chase taunted, "Don't know the number? Would you like me to dial it for you?"

Charbonnet glared at him. "I'll dial it myself. From *my* office, you smug son-of-a-bitch. And when I finish, you're going to find yourself out of a job and your ass being shipped back to New Jersey or wherever it is you come from."

"Don't count on it, Charbonnet. I'm here until the renovations are finished and this place is back on its feet. Considering the poor job that's been done of managing it, that's liable to be some time."

"This is still *my* hotel and I want you out of here," Charbonnet snapped, his face nearly purple with rage.

Stunned by her father's angry outburst, Madeline froze in the doorway leading into Chase's offices. Closing the door to the suite, she looked over at Ellen who quickly buried her nose in a stack of files.

"And until you're gone, I want you to keep away from my daughter."

Madeline's breath caught in her throat. She felt the color rush to her cheeks and hurried to the partially opened door.

"Then you've got another problem. Because I have absolutely no intention of staying away from Madeline," Chase said, his voice as hard and cold as his face. "My relationship with her is none of your business."

"Like hell it isn't. She's still my daughter, and I won't have people talking about her because you—"

"Father!" Madeline rushed into the room, mortified as much by her father's warning off Chase as by the ugly flush of color staining his cheeks. She pushed the door closed behind her and went over to her father. "What on earth is going on here? Why are you fighting with Chase?"

"Stay out of this, Madeline," he father said. "It doesn't concern you."

"Doesn't concern me?" Madeline repeated, bristling at the dismissal. "Since I, and anyone within shouting distance, just heard you tell Chase to keep away from me, I'd say it does concern me."

"You're only a small part of it. It's business, Madeline. You wouldn't understand."

Madeline checked the urge to flinch. It had always been this way. Her father not believing her capable of understanding or running the hotel as a business. He had already demonstrated that much by opting to sell off a share of the hotel, hadn't he? So, why should it hurt to have him say as much now? It shouldn't. But it did. "You might be surprised just how much I am capable of understanding about business," she told him, unable to keep the hurt out of her voice.

Her father sighed. Under the glare of the office lighting, she could easily define each line and groove in his face. Today he looked every one of his sixty-three years, she thought. Was it her imagination, or were there more of those age lines than had been there a month ago? Suddenly Madeline felt swamped by thoughts of his mortality. "Father, I—"

"Just leave it alone, Madeline. You worry about straightening things out between you and Bradley." He touched her cheek, stroking it as he had when she was a little girl and had awakened from a bad dream. "You let me worry about the hotel."

His gaze flitted back to Chase and all the tenderness of a moment ago vanished. Moving back to the desk, he picked up the crumpled letter lying there. "You haven't heard the last of this, McAllister—not by any means."

"I didn't think I had."

He marched over to the door and pulled it open. "Are you coming, Madeline?"

She hesitated, torn between her concern for her father and her desire to remain with Chase.

"Go ahead, Madeline," Chase told her, making the decision for her. She would have sworn she saw disappointment in his eyes.

"But I had a message you wanted to see me."

"I do. But it can wait. You know where to find me. You get back to me when you're ready," he told her.

Heat shimmied its way up her cheeks. She hadn't missed the meaning behind the words or the message in those icy blue eyes before he'd turned his back on her and her father and buzzed for his secretary.

Chase was angry. He was tired of playing the game. He wanted her and knew she wanted him. And if and when she was ready to take him as her lover, she would have to take the next step. Madeline swallowed hard at the thought as she followed her father out of the office.

"Stay away from him, Madeline," her father told her as they stepped inside the elevator. "Don't be taken in by that so-called charm of his. Chase McAllister's the wrong man for you."

Unfortunately, she thought as the doors closed and the old elevator made its way down to the lobby, Chase McAllister was the only man she wanted.

But if Chase still wanted her, he gave no indication. She could have kissed him for not gloating over her father, when Majestic had firmly sided with Chase on the issue of the interior decorator for the hotel. But in the two weeks since she had left his office with her father, he hadn't given her the opportunity. Nor had he tried to coax her into his bed.

Madeline frowned. When they had been alone for scant seconds before a staff meeting, he'd made no attempt to steal a kiss. There had been no calls from him demanding she come to his office. There had been no further requests for her to join him for dinner or even coffee.

And she had missed those stolen kisses. She had missed the trumped-up excuses to see her. She had missed *him,* Madeline admitted. She far preferred the arrogant, flirtatious Chase to this stranger who treated her with cool professionalism—and who seemed to go out of his way to avoid being alone with her.

You know where to find me, Madeline. You get back to me when you're ready.

Well, she was ready.

Madeline swallowed the lump of nerves lodged in her throat. Edgy, she crushed the skirt of her dress in her fist, then smoothed the black silk with her fingertips as she strode purposefully through the lobby to the elevators. She had been ready for more than a week and would have made the trip to Chase's room sooner had it not been for her father. While her father had always spent less time than he should at the hotel, since his battle and loss to Chase on the decorating issue, his presence had grown even more scarce. Even though Chase was technically at the helm of hotel operations and had gained most everyone's respect, the employees, for the most part, still considered the hotel to be the property of the Charbonnet family. Old habits and loyalties didn't die easily.

Hence, in her father's absence, it was to her they turned for the everyday decision making or to handle any daily crises that arose. While she didn't mind, it did eat into her time—especially considering she had her own job functions to perform in the sales and marketing departments.

Perhaps it was just as well, she decided. Watching the floor numbers register, she waited to see which of the two elevators would make it down to the lobby first. Given her father's strange mood of late and his unsuccessful attempts to get her and Bradley back together again, she wasn't exactly his favorite person at the moment. No doubt, her approval rating as a daughter would take another dip when she finally did convince him that he was wasting his time where she and Bradley were concerned. He certainly wouldn't be happy when she told him the reason she would never marry Bradley was because she was already in love with Chase.

Her stomach somersaulted, just as it had when she had first come to that realization last week. She had been hit smack dab in the belly when she'd watched him help Ruthie with a heavy tray in the restaurant. The same feeling had hit her later, when she'd heard he'd given instructions that no waiter or waitress was to have their serving trays overloaded. At the staff meeting, there had been genuine affection and excitement in his eyes when he had shown old photos of the hotel and outlined the painstaking effort that had been undertaken to not change the hotel, but to restore it to its former beauty. She had known then that he loved her hotel as much as she did. And the kick in her belly had promptly moved straight to her heart.

She loved him. While Chase might not love her, he did want her. And for now it would have to be enough. Her mother had once told her that the Saint Charles was a magical place—a place designed for lovers and for the celebration of love. Considering her parents' devotion to each other and her father's continued love for her mother despite her death years ago, perhaps it was true. Perhaps some of that magic would rub off on her and Chase. At any rate she intended to find out, Madeline told herself and pushed the button again, knowing it wouldn't speed up the slow-descending elevator cars, but doing it all the same.

"I'm sorry, sir. But you didn't guarantee the reservation with a credit card or a check. We held the room until six o'clock, and when you weren't here, the room was released."

Madeline's gaze swiveled to the front desk where a middle-aged man, with his suitcase and briefcase resting beside him, stood glowering at the desk clerk. From the man's rumpled suit and the weary lines of his face, she surmised he had just had one of those travel days from hell. Finding his hotel reservation canceled had evidently been the last straw.

"And I'm telling you my flight was delayed. I couldn't get here before six. I made that reservation months ago, and I want a room. Now," the irate man demanded.

"I'm sorry, Mr. Addison. But all we have left are suites. The hotel's almost filled up for one of the university graduations. As I explained, I can put you in a suite, but not at a king room rate."

"Listen to me, young man." He leaned over the front desk and glowered at the clerk. "I come to this hotel several times a year, and I was planning to come back next month with my wife for a vacation, but if you can't—"

"Hello, Mr. Addison. Madeline Charbonnet, sales director for the Saint Charles." She extended her hand. "We're glad to have you visiting us again. What seems to be the problem, Marvin?"

While the desk clerk went through a brief recap and Addison rehashed his travel day, Madeline made sympathetic noises as she surveyed the rooming list for weekend arrivals and departures. She queried Mr. Addison about his airline departure schedule, and after juggling with the guest arrivals scheduled for the following day, she turned back to the clerk. "Marvin, put Mr. Addison in Suite 503 and charge him the king room rate. Have housekeeping put his room first on the list for cleanup." That way the suite would be ready for the late arrivals she had slated for the room. "Enjoy your stay with us, Mr. Addison."

"I will. Thank you, Ms. Charbonnet," Addison told her, his face filled with relief.

"We'll look forward to having you and your wife join us next month. Perhaps you'd like Marvin to make your reservation for you now."

"I'll do that. And I'll guarantee it this time with my credit card. Thank you again."

"My pleasure," she assured him. Marvin mouthed the words *thank you* and she gave him a wink, while Mr. Addison fished out his credit card and gave the clerk the dates for his trip next month.

"Very smooth, Princess."

Madeline whipped around at the sound of Chase's voice. Her heart stammered in her chest to find him standing behind her.

"It seems there's just no end to your talents. You're able to soothe even the most irate guests with your charm—even when it's not your job to do so."

Madeline's breath caught in her throat. Excitement clawed its way up her spine. There was nothing soothing or the least bit charming about the hot, hungry light in his eyes as he looked at her. His gaze raked over her, stripping her bare of the black dress she had worn specifically with the intention of seducing him. An answering heat caught fire inside her.

"Madeline," Marvin called over to her from the front desk. "The couple in 905 wants to stay an extra day, but we're sold out for tomorrow. Do you think you could take another look at the rooming list and see if—"

Chase shot a silencing glance at the clerk. Anger seemed to vibrate from him. "You handle it, Marvin. Ms. Charbonnet's not on duty."

"Chase, I don't mind. Really." She offered him a nervous smile.

"But *I* do." Before she could protest further, he cupped her arm and marched her outside to the street. "Where's your car?" he asked, his voice razor sharp.

"In the hotel garage," she replied, confused by his obvious annoyance.

"Come on, then. I'll see you to your car. You should have been gone from here hours ago."

"But I did go home. To change clothes."

His gaze swept over her again. "Then you should have stayed home."

"I didn't want to stay home." Madeline stopped in the middle of the sidewalk to look at him and tell him she had come back to see him. A sliver of moonlight, combined with the faint glow from a street lamp, emphasized the rigid line of his jaw and the muscle ticking angrily in his cheek. The anger confused her, sent the nerves climbing through her stomach again. She took a deep breath. "I came back because I wanted—"

"Because you wanted to cover for your father again," he said, his voice filled with disgust. "You've been doing it since the first week I got here."

"Chase, why are you so angry with me?"

"Why shouldn't I be angry? You wear yourself out. You spend twice the number of hours here that you should, picking up your father's slack just so he can go out to his dinner parties and society affairs. Did you think I hadn't noticed that it's gotten worse these past two weeks? That he's never here anymore and that you're covering for him?"

Not giving her a chance to answer, he caught her arm and hustled her into the garage. "I've had it, Madeline. I don't care if he is your father or how much you love him, you're not going to do it anymore. You're going home. Now. And you're going to stay there until Monday morning."

"I have no intention of spending my weekend locked up in my cottage."

"Then don't. Do whatever it is you want to do, as long as it doesn't include working here. I don't want to see you back inside the hotel before Monday morning." He stopped inside the dark, empty garage. "Where's your car."

Madeline pointed to the far corner where she had parked, and he began to march her down the long, dark lane, her heels clicking loudly on the pavement in the silent garage as they approached her car. His anger still made no sense to her, but she refused to let it and his apparent irritation with her father deter her from telling him she had changed her mind. That she was ready for them to become lovers. "Chase, I know my father's absence has been a problem. But I didn't come back tonight because of him. I came back to the hotel because—"

"Damn it, Madeline. Stop covering for the man."

"I'm not covering for him, you idiot. I'm trying to tell you—"

"You're trying to make excuses for him. When are you going to open your eyes and stop denying that he's done a lousy job of running the hotel?" Chase snapped. Grabbing her by the shoulders, he gave her a gentle shake and backed her up against the wall.

Madeline hiked up her chin, squared her shoulders, causing her breasts to thrust forward.

His blue eyes glittered with fury and frustration.

And desire.

Madeline watched it catch, then burst into flame as he became aware of her body gently grazing against his. "When are you going to stop denying us?" he asked, his voice whiskey rough and taut with pain.

"I'm not denying us. Not anymore." Reaching up, she ran her fingers down the curve of his jaw, traced the angry scar along his chin. She met his gaze. "That's what I've been trying to tell you."

He caught her hand, trapped it between them. Heat flickered in his eyes, threatening to engulf them both. "What are you saying?"

"I'm saying *you're* the reason I came back to the hotel tonight. I was on my way to your room."

"Why?"

She placed her palms on either side of his face, then slid her fingers up into his hair. She pulled his mouth down to within inches of hers. "Because I want you, Chase," she told him. "All of you. Or however much you're willing to give me."

She didn't wait for him to answer, to outline the parameters of their affair. She had done enough thinking for both of them. Too much time had already been wasted. She wanted— She needed Chase.

She took his mouth then, as he had so often taken hers. Hungrily, greedily, she nipped at his lower lip and slid her tongue between his teeth to invade, to taste, to torment.

A part of her registered the cool steel of the garage wall at her back, the mingling scents of dampness, exhaust fumes and gasoline. The unique scent of soap and spice and male that she associated with Chase. Anyone from the hotel could walk in at any moment and see them. She couldn't seem to bring herself to care. She deepened the kiss.

A guttural sound escaped from Chase as he hauled her against him. He was rock hard and deeply aroused—and she was the cause. Excitement, fear, pleasure raced through Madeline. He ravished her with his mouth, with his hands, sending the flames of desire licking through her body.

At the sound of approaching voices and footsteps, Chase broke off the kiss. Swearing, he crushed her against him. The sound of their own labored breathing seemed to echo in the darkness around them.

"We can go back to my place or your hotel room. I'd prefer my place," Madeline finally managed. Pulling back, she handed him her keys.

Chase glanced over at her car and then back at her. His mouth curved into that slow, wicked grin, but the hunger never left his eyes. "Assuming I can make it that far."

Ten

He made it to Madeline's cottage—but just barely, Chase admitted, as he shoved the key into the lock of her front door with shaky fingers. It had taken every ounce of control he possessed not to pull the car over on the first dark street he had come to and make love to her right then and there in the front seat.

Chase's lips tightened at the notion. Just went to show how close to the edge he was these days. He hadn't made love in the seat of a car since he had been an overanxious teenager with raging hormones and lacking any ounce of finesse or sensitivity for his partner. And even then he couldn't remember feeling this...this desperation, this primitive need to claim a woman with his body.

But then again, none of the females he had known as a young man or any of the women he had encountered since had been Madeline. Cutting a glance to her, Chase took in the lush curves beneath the silk dress, her slightly swollen lips. He shifted his gaze to hers. Her green eyes shimmered with liquid heat as she looked at him.

Desire streaked through him with the speed of a comet, making his gut tighten with anticipation as he thought of wrapping himself in that heat. He turned the key and jerked on the doorknob, but the lock wouldn't give.

"Do you need some help?" Madeline whispered, her voice a husky purr that danced along his spine and conjured images of soft, naked skin, silken sheets and hot sex. She moved closer to him, her breast lightly brushing the side of his arm.

The innocent contact zapped through him and went straight to his loins. Chase dropped the key. Cursing his unsteady fingers, he scooped up the key, jammed it into the lock a second time and twisted. The door swung open.

Madeline slipped inside, and Chase hurried in behind her. Before he had closed the door, he was reaching for her. She laughed and came to him, with that siren's smile on her lips and that womanly gleam in her eyes that said she knew all about his fantasies, that she had fantasies, too. She lifted her face to him, offering him her lips and whatever else he dared to take.

Chase crushed her to him. He captured her tempting mouth, devouring it with a need that would have frightened him if he had been able to think. But he couldn't think. He could only feel and taste. That incredibly sweet and drugging combination of fire and ice, of innocence and sin. He couldn't get enough of her taste. He couldn't get enough of her.

She pushed against his chest, tearing her lips free. "Chase," she gasped as he relinquished her mouth.

The breathless sound of his name on her lips pushed him closer to the edge. Chase kissed her neck, tasting the soft scented skin as he worked his way to her ear. He grazed the delicate shell of her lobe with his tongue, delighting at the sudden hitch in her breath.

His own breath hitched when she repeated the action, when that clever mouth of hers kissed the lobe of his ear, nipped it with sharp teeth. Then he felt himself being pushed against the door, while those slim graceful fingers of hers went to work, loosening his tie, pulling it free from his collar and throwing it to the floor.

She moved swiftly. With an urgency that surprised him, excited him. She reached for the top button of his shirt at the same time she reached for his mouth. Chase opened to her, welcoming the invading thrust of her tongue and the dueling ritual that followed. His heart thundered like a racehorse at the finish line on Derby day as her fingers trailed a searing path of heat down his chest, where she continued to fight with the buttons of his shirt.

He had dreamed of her like this, wild and wanton in his arms. Chase moaned as her fingernails scored his bared skin before continuing to open his shirt. His body on fire from her touch, Chase deepened the kiss. He ran his hands down her sides, skimming the swell of her breasts with his fingertips, exploring the indentation at her waist, the full curve of her hips.

Madeline broke the kiss. Her breasts heaved beneath the black silk as she drew air into her lungs. Her eyes were emerald flames as they raced from his face to his partially opened shirt. She ripped the fabric open, scattering the remaining buttons to the floor as she pulled the shirt free from his slacks. She dragged it off him, tossed it to the floor with the buttons.

Then her hands were on him. Those soft elegant hands were running over his chest, down his belly, unbuckling his belt, fussing with the snap on his slacks, tugging at his zipper. Her fingers brushed against his shaft.

Chase groaned. He cupped her bottom, jerked her body against his aching hardness and seized her mouth once more. He ravaged her mouth, allowed her to ravage him. He was ruthless. So was she.

When she squeezed his buttocks, Chase nearly exploded. He pulled his mouth free. Sweet heaven, he thought, sucking air into his lungs. He struggled for some measure of control. He found none. He had made it back to her house, but he wasn't at all sure he'd be able make it to the bedroom. Not when he was within inches of taking her right now in the dimly lit hallway.

Quickly, before he did just that, he scooped her up in his arms in a movement that sent her high heels thudding to the wooden floor. "Where's your bedroom?" he demanded roughly.

"End of the hall," she murmured, wrapping her arms around his neck, while her mouth made an erogenous zone of his shoulder. Her teeth bit into his flesh and Chase shuddered.

Kicking the door open, he stepped inside her bedroom. He was only vaguely aware of the smell of roses, of walking across thick carpet into a room draped in swaths of vanilla and pale rose silk. A rice bed covered in that same shade of pale rose dominated the room.

A lady's boudoir. The thought flitted in and out of his consciousness as quick as a heartbeat. He stopped in front of the four-poster bed. Madeline slid to her feet, torturing him with the feel of her body against his.

And then he was beyond thinking. He was beyond anything but the desperate need to feel Madeline beneath him, to feel himself inside her, to hear her cry out his name as he filled her. Desire shuddered through him. He wanted to take her now, to sheathe himself inside her warmth with one powerful thrust and end the months of torment. And she would let him. The wild hunger in her eyes, the frantic pulse beating at her throat told him she would.

But he wanted more. So much more than that swift release. He wanted to fan that flame inside her, watch it catch and burst into a blaze in those expressive eyes. And when it was white-hot, when her desire for him was raging out of control, he wanted to dive into the flame with her and take her with him.

"You're wearing too many clothes," he told her, his voice savage with need. In seconds he had the dress off and feasted on the sight of her body covered by scraps of black lace. He had dreamed of that body, had imagined seeing that soft cream skin like this. The reality was even better than his dreams.

Madeline's hands clutched at his hips. Her body trembled. "Chase, please . . . Touch me."

Desire licked through him again, singeing him with its heat. Then he touched her. First with his hands. And then with his mouth. He touched and tasted, following the curve of her jaw, the slender column of her neck, the valley between her breasts. He flicked open the clasp at the front of her bra and filled his palms with her breasts.

Forcing himself to go slowly, Chase skimmed his fingertips over the dark rosy tips and smiled as they pebbled and pouted beneath his touch. Lowering his head, he took one nipple between his teeth.

Madeline cried out. Her fingernails dug into his bare shoulders. She arched her body toward him. Chase scraped his jaw across her breasts, worrying the stubble of his beard would mark her sensitive skin, but unable to stop himself. Like a marauder, he bit. He suckled. He laved that exquisite flesh with his tongue, fed by her cries of pleasure and the pressure of her fingers tangled in his hair.

And then she was dragging his face up to hers, nipping at his neck, his jaw, his bottom lip as her mouth and teeth raced over him. She clawed at his slacks, her fingers scraping against his bulging shaft as she fought with his zipper. Chase kicked off his shoes and helped her tug down his pants, kicking them and his shorts over to join her dress and bra.

Chase lifted her to the bed, then quickly joined her there. He kissed her again, ravishing her with his mouth as she had ravished him. Pulling his mouth free, he ran his hand down her rib cage, felt the quiver go through her when his fingers raced over her stomach to rest at the edge of her panties. He stared at the scrap of black lace shielding her from him and ripped it in two.

Madeline gasped. Her eyes widened. Fear flickered in their depths for a moment. It excited him. It made him feel guilty. It made him want her even more. He slid a finger inside her. She was hot and wet and ready for him. His body shook as he fought for control.

"I wanted to be gentle. To go slow. But I can't. I want you too much." He spat out the admission.

"I don't want gentle or slow," she told him. "All I want is you."

His control broke. He sheathed himself in her with one powerful thrust. He heard Madeline's breath snag, watched her eyes glaze with heat.

And then she was clutching his hips, arching her body, meeting his thrusts. He felt the first climax rip into her, watched the shock of it register in her eyes. His own body shuddered with her release. Wanting to prolong her pleasure, he swallowed her protests as he withdrew almost completely and entered her again.

"Chase...please," she cried out. Her nails dug into his back. She bit at his lip, his jaw, his neck. He felt the sting of her teeth as they sank into his shoulder. Another climax shook her, blasted through her body like a jolt of lightning and straight through to him.

Chase slammed into her again, burying himself to the hilt in her sweet heat. The blood pounded in his ears. He heard Madeline call out his name again. And then the flames exploded around him, inside him, devouring him with fiery tongues. Grabbing Madeline's hips, he cried out in triumph and dived after her into the blaze.

Madeline opened her eyes and stretched, wincing slightly at the protest of sore muscles. She glanced over at the window where morning light snuck past the damask drapes to dance like fireflies in the still-darkened room.

The clock on the bedside table read 9:40 a.m. How decadent, Madeline thought with amusement, unable to recall the last time she had slept so late on a Saturday morning. But then, she had spent very little of the night actually sleeping. Chase had seen to that. She stretched again and smiled at the pleasant ache that ran through her body.

Chase stirred beside her. His hair-roughened leg brushed against her bare thigh, setting off tiny shivers of memory and effectively reminding her that she was naked. A flush stole over her body, and she tugged the sheet up around her breasts as she recalled how wanton she had been with him.

"Do you always blush so beautifully in the morning?" Chase asked, his deep voice making her heart kick as he leaned over and kissed her softly, slowly on the mouth. He lifted his head and traced the line of her lips, her cheekbone, to the shell of her ear, then started back down to her neck. His fingers lingered at the edge of the sheet just above her breasts. He looked into her eyes, amusement in his expression. "Even your ears are a delightful shade of pink. Makes me curious to see just how far that blush extends."

Madeline batted his hand away and anchored the sheet more securely. "You're not going to find out."

He gave her that wicked grin, and her stomach did its usual flutter kick. "Not even the reason for the blush?"

"Forget it, Chase. I have no intention of feeding that ego of yours."

"It's not my ego that needs feeding," he told her huskily. His eyes darkened as he looked at her, touching her like a caress. He kissed her shoulder, moved to her collarbone. "You were incredible last night, Princess."

Madeline felt the blush again, but was helpless to stop it. "I . . . I've never been that way before," she told him honestly. "I felt so . . . so—"

"So what?" he asked, capturing the fingers that clung to the sheet and bringing them to his lips.

"So wild . . . so wanton."

"I like you wild and wanton." He peeled away the sheet and Madeline could feel the heat curl in her stomach, pool between her thighs as he stared at her breasts. He lifted those hot blue eyes to hers. "I want you that way again. Now."

Madeline's heart jumped as his mouth skimmed the curve of her breast. His tongue flicked back and forth over one nipple and then the other while his hand eased down her stomach, beneath the sheet, between her thighs. He tested her with his fingers, coaxed the sensitive nub at her center. Relentlessly he took her over one peak and then another and another until her body quivered and she cried out his name and begged him for more.

"Tell me what you want, Madeline. Tell me," he said roughly, pinning her with the savage heat in those blue eyes as he stripped away the sheet and moved between her thighs. His golden body loomed over her, hot and hard and ready. "Tell me," he demanded.

"You," she told him boldly, her breath coming fast and furious. Feeling every bit the wild and wanton creature she had confessed to earlier, she opened and drew him to her. "I want you."

And she still wanted him, Madeline admitted Monday morning as she poured the hot milk into her cup and reached for the coffee. She added the dark brew to the milk, creating the café au lait she adored. Only now, after spending the better part of the weekend with Chase, both in and out of bed, the wanting had turned to something deeper. Something far more dangerous than a simple affair.

Sighing, Madeline measured one spoon of sugar into the coffee. She thought about her hips for the briefest of seconds and added another scoop of sugar anyway. Who was she kidding? She mocked in silence her poor attempt at self-deception. She had known from the outset that an affair with Chase would be anything but simple. And she had known in her heart and had even admitted to herself, when she had gone looking for him at the hotel that night, that she was already halfway in love with him.

She let out another deep sigh and stirred her coffee. She just hadn't expected to fall the rest of the way so quickly. Or all alone. And from all indications she had done just that— tumbled headfirst for a man who proclaimed to have no roots and to not want any.

Well, what did you expect, Madeline? When did you ever go into anything using logic instead of your heart? She'd put her soul into learning the hotel business despite her father's disapproval. And he'd opted to sell off a chunk of the hotel rather than give her a chance to prove she could run it. And she'd known from the first time she'd set eyes on Chase McAllister that he was a threat to her, not only to her dream of running the Saint Charles but to her heart, as well. But she'd foolishly convinced herself she could love Chase, indulge in a quick affair with him and still manage to walk away with her heart.

No question about it, Madeline. You're a certified idiot. Disgusted with herself, Madeline took a sip of her coffee and reached for more sugar. It was time this idiot started exercising some common sense, she decided. And she'd start by cutting her losses now—before Chase discovered just how badly she had fallen.

"Is that coffee I smell?"

Madeline jerked, her spoon clanging against the china cup. "Sure is. Would you like a cup?" she returned, pleased at how calm she had managed to sound. Forcing a smile on her lips, she turned around to face him.

"Love some. But I'll get it. You go ahead and finish yours."

He strolled into her kitchen with only a towel draped around his hips, as though it were the most natural thing in the world. His hair was still damp from the shower, and she could see the nick to his cheek, no doubt courtesy of her razor. Spotting the teeth marks on his shoulder, Madeline jerked her gaze back to his face and caught the devil gleam in his eyes. She spun around and busied herself setting out another cup and saucer on the countertop.

"Better yet," Chase murmured coming up behind her. He snagged an arm around her waist and kissed the back of her neck, then turned her to face him.

Madeline's eyes fluttered closed as he lowered his head. He kissed her slowly, tenderly, taking what seemed an eternity to taste every inch of her mouth, until her entire being seemed centered on the mating of their lips. So drugged was she by the feel of his mouth that she was barely aware that he had unbuttoned the jacket of her suit and was working on the pearl studs of her blouse until she heard one of the pearl backings hit the tile floor. Madeline jerked her mouth free and opened her eyes.

"Why don't we forget about the coffee and go back to bed?" he coaxed, kissing the base of her throat that he had exposed.

"We can't. We have to go to work," she protested even as the first ripples of desire began to gather in her. She clung to his shoulders as he moved to her neck.

"I'm the boss, remember. I say let's play hooky." His hands gave up on her blouse and started in on her skirt while his mouth zeroed in on her ear.

It was the hiss of her zipper that brought Madeline to her senses. Ducking under his arm, she scurried across the kitchen. With shaky fingers she went about refastening her clothes and renewed her resolve to get out while she still could. "Chase, I think we need to talk about our... about what happened between us this weekend."

He grinned at her, that wicked, knee-weakening grin. "You mean the fact that I think you're the most sensual woman I've ever known and despite a weekend of mind-boggling sex with you, I want you again?"

Madeline flushed from the root of her head to the tips of her toes. "I mean we never really discussed our... well, our relationship."

"All right." He poured himself a cup of coffee, added milk and stirred in sugar. "So let's discuss it."

Her stomach in knots, Madeline took a deep breath and began, "I wouldn't want the fact that we're...that now that we've had sex, for it to affect our working relationship."

"It won't," he assured her.

"But it could. If word got out at the hotel that we were having an affair, it could hurt both of our careers."

Chase set down his cup. The devil gleam disappeared in his eyes. So did his smile. "Cut to the chase, Princess. Exactly what is it you're trying to say?"

"I'm saying we wanted each other and we went to bed together. We satisfied our curiosity. And even though this weekend has been a...a wonderful diversion for both of us, now it's time for us to go back to the real world."

"A diversion? Is that what it was for you?"

Madeline tipped up her chin. "All right. Sex with you was an earth-shattering experience. No doubt it'll rank right up there at the top of the list as my most memorable affair. Satisfied?"

"Not even close. And despite that prim little brush-off speech, I don't think you're satisfied, either."

She eyed him warily while struggling to keep her heartbeat steady. "So what is it you're saying?"

"I'm saying I want more." He spit out the words and moved in, trapping her against the refrigerator. "A lot more."

"Then you...you want to continue our affair?" she asked, her heart scrambling with hope that it was more than an affair he wanted.

His eyes narrowed. "Don't you?"

"Yes," Madeline admitted. "But I think we need to set down some parameters for our, um, our relationship."

"You mean you want to set up guidelines?"

Feeling somewhat foolish, Madeline pushed away Chase's arm and walked over to the counter to fuss with the coffee. "Yes. I think it's the sensible thing to do."

"All right." Chase leaned against the counter and folded his arms over his chest. "So exactly what are these guidelines you expect us to follow?"

Madeline tore her gaze away from the attractive picture he made, standing in her kitchen wearing only a towel and that amused smile on his lips. "Well, for one, as long as we're involved with each other, I expect our physical relationship to be exclusive."

"Not a problem, since I have no intention of sharing you," he told her. "Like I told you, I've never quite gotten the knack of sharing anything I considered mine. And make no mistake, Princess. I *do* consider you mine."

Madeline swallowed. A flurry of excitement danced along her spine. "It works both ways, McAllister."

"Selfish, too, huh?" he asked, laughter in his eyes. "I always did think that rule about sharing was overrated. But don't worry, you won't be sharing me with anyone, darling."

Reaching for her, Chase pulled her against him. "Because I haven't been able to even think about another woman since I met you."

Another seed of hope sprouted inside Madeline. She struggled to temper that hope with logic, telling herself that having an affair with her didn't mean Chase would fall in love with her.

"What else?" he asked, unfastening the buttons of her jacket again while he kissed the corner of her mouth.

"We agree to be discreet," she whispered huskily as she began to succumb to the magic of his touch.

Chase's lips stilled. His fingers stalled at the neck of her blouse. He pulled back a fraction and stared into her eyes. "You mean keep our relationship secret?"

"Well, I hadn't exactly thought of it in those terms. But yes, I suppose keeping our involvement a secret would probably be a good idea."

"And convenient, I bet."

"Probably," Madeline agreed, mildly annoyed at his eagerness to accept her offer to keep their relationship under wraps. But annoyance aside, the suggestion made sense—especially for her. She sighed. "I guess it would be. Sometimes I forget just what a small city New Orleans can be. And despite the city's wild, party image, there are a lot of old-fashioned values at work here. You're probably right. It wouldn't serve any purpose for people to think of us as a couple. That would only lead to complications."

"Complications for whom?"

"Why, for both of us," Madeline replied, puzzled as much by the edge in his voice as by the shift of undercurrents coming from Chase. "You have your position at the hotel to consider and I...I have my family and my friends."

"And heaven forbid that your father or your friends find out you and I were sleeping together."

Madeline flushed at the reminder of what their relationship was based upon. "I don't see what purpose it would serve to publicize the fact. I haven't had very many relationships with men," Madeline confessed. She forced herself to meet that cool, blue gaze of his. "The people who know me well may not understand. They would more than likely think things are more serious between us than they are. They'd have expectations. And I'd just as soon not have to give them any explanations when you go back to New Jersey in a few months and things between us end.''

"What if I don't want things to be over between us when my job here ends? What if I'm interested in more than a brief fling?''

"Are you?'' Madeline asked, praying he didn't hear that quiver of hope in her voice.

"No,'' Chase told her.

He wasn't looking for more than a fling, Chase reminded himself. A brief affair with Madeline was all that he had ever intended. He should be happy that she wasn't looking for anything more than that. So why in the hell did it leave an acid feeling in his gut?

"Fine. Since you're staying in the hotel, meeting there won't work. I suggest we meet here at my place when we want to be together. That way we exercise discretion and avoid anything that might publicize our involvement.''

Madeline had just offered him a dream affair. Hot sex with a classy and beautiful woman whom he both liked and admired. A relationship with no strings. No commitments. It was tailor-made for him. And it held as much appeal for him as a trip to the dentist's office.

"Then we're agreed?''

"No.'' Chase ground out the word, furious with Madeline for her sensible suggestions and with himself for being hurt by them. "I don't agree.'' Despite his successes and the fact that he had made something of himself, listening to Madeline's cool approach to their affair reawakened feelings he had long since buried. He felt like the boy he had been—the kid at St. Mark's no one had wanted, the one who had been skipped over for adoption, the one who had been left behind each holiday, the sorry little kid whose mother hadn't loved him enough to live.

"I may agree not to make love to you on my desk with everyone watching, but I'll be damned if I'm going to sneak around corners to see you and pretend there's nothing going on between us when there is.''

"But, Chase—''

"No buts, Madeline. If I'm not good enough to be seen with you in public, to share a dinner table with you and your pedigreed friends, then I guess I'm not good enough to share your bed, either."

Madeline blinked. Her green eyes widened with astonishment. "That's not how I feel! Where on earth did you get the idea that I was ashamed of you?"

"From you. Isn't that what that little speech of yours was about? Isn't that the reason you decided we need a list of guidelines for an affair?"

She shook her head. "Oh, Chase. That's not how I feel. Not at all. How could you even think such a thing?" She touched his cheek. "I was simply trying to save us both from what will probably be some awkward questions if people start seeing us together as a couple."

The sick feeling in his stomach began to ease. Chase captured her fingers, brought them to his lips. "Princess, I'm not worried about what people will think or say if they find out we're seeing each other. The truth is, I doubt that anyone's going to be particularly surprised. Not even Paul or Chloe. I haven't exactly made a secret of my attraction to you."

"I wasn't thinking about them so much as my father, Chase. I know the two of you haven't been seeing eye-to-eye lately. I don't know how he'll feel about the idea of us being together."

"My guess is he won't like it," Chase told her honestly. He didn't want to think about Henri Charbonnet. He didn't want to think about the possible complications his affair with Madeline would pose to his plans to destroy the man.

"You're probably right. But not just because it's you. Except for my brief engagement to Bradley, my father's always stressed that I should never mix hotel and business relationships with personal ones. He thinks it's an unwise practice and doesn't believe in it."

Maybe not now, Chase mused silently. But Henri Charbonnet had believed in doing so at one time. Long enough to break a young woman's heart and make her take her own life. "I want you, but I don't want to make you unhappy by causing trouble between you and your father. If you want to end things, tell me now. I won't like it, but I'll understand."

She answered by linking her arms around his neck and kissing him long, deep and slow. When she released his mouth, she said, "I don't want to end things, Chase. Not unless you do. But I should warn you, my father might try to make things difficult for you. You know he's already called the head of Majestic Hotels to complain about you. I can't imagine what would happen if he told them that you and I were having an affair."

"If they saw you, they'd think I was lucky," he quipped, trying to wipe the concern from her eyes. "You let me worry about Majestic and your father. Neither of them has anything to do with the way I feel about you or with the way you make me feel."

He kissed her neck and shoulder. He ran his hands down her spine, over her hips, her bottom, along the back of her thighs. He eased his fingers under the hem of her skirt and started to work his way back up.

Madeline gasped. Her body trembled beneath his touch. "Tell me how I make you feel, Chase."

Heat shot through him, hardening his loins. He hiked up her skirt the rest of the way and jerked away his towel. "I'll do better than that, Princess. I'll show you."

Eleven

"**Y**ou're sleeping with him, aren't you?"

Madeline nearly choked on the forkful of romaine lettuce at Chloe's question. With effort, she managed to swallow and calmly put down her fork. Bringing her napkin to her mouth, she stole a quick glance in the direction Chase had been headed and breathed a sigh of relief that he was out of earshot of their table. "Just who is the 'him' you're referring to?" Madeline asked, striving to sound casual while meeting the other woman's knowing gaze.

Chloe made a snorting sound that would have sent her friend's ladylike mother into a tailspin. "Chase McAllister. That's who."

In the two months since they had begun their affair, she and Chase had maintained the discretion factor they had both agreed upon. She saw no reason to alter things now. Especially when Chase would soon be leaving. Pushing aside the sick feeling that came whenever she thought about Chase's exit from her life, Madeline reached for her glass of iced tea. "What on earth would give you an idea like that?"

"Gee, I don't know." Chloe plucked a cherry tomato from her plate with her fingers and bit into it, her mouth spreading into a Cheshire cat grin. "Probably had something to do with the way the two of you devour each other with your eyes when you think no one's looking."

"Really, Chloe. You've been watching too many soaps. It's got your imagination working overtime."

Chloe shook her head. "Nope. It's not my imagination. The two of you are lovers. I've had my suspicions for a while, but I wasn't sure until a few minutes ago."

Madeline shifted in her seat. She skirted a quick glance at the party at the table next to hers and was grateful they were engaged in their own conversation.

"Oh for goodness sakes, quit squirming, Maddie, and tell me the truth."

Madeline leaned over and glared at her friend. "Would you please keep your voice down?"

"All right," Chloe whispered. "But it is true, isn't it?"

Madeline's brain scrambled for a convincing lie. She found none. What good would it do her to deny it? "Yes," Madeline returned, sighing. "It's true."

Chloe's hand smacked the table. "I knew it! I told Paul so a month ago, and he didn't believe me. Wait until he finds out I was right!"

Madeline squeezed her eyes shut a moment and prayed for strength. When she opened them again, she said, "I would think with a new baby the two of you would have more important things to do than speculate about my love life."

"Oh, we do," Chloe informed her. Riffling through her salad, the dark-haired pixie speared an olive and beamed. "Problem is when you're both worn out from two o'clock feedings, the spirit may be willing, but not always the body. So speculating on your friends' love lives can be a nice substitute."

Madeline toyed with her salad, then pushed it aside. "Is it that obvious, Chloe? I mean about me and Chase?"

"Only to anybody with eyes in their head."

Madeline bit back a groan.

"Hey, lighten up, Maddie." Chloe patted her hand. "I'm only teasing. I'll admit I've been picking up undercurrents about the two of you since day one, but I wasn't sure things had moved beyond the lust stage until he came over to the table a few minutes ago. I would have even discounted the steamy looks that passed between you two. But it was the body language that cinched it for me."

"The body language?"

"Uh hmm. When Chase declined the offer for tea and said he wanted water instead. You passed him your glass."

"So?"

"So a few minutes later he was talking about the progression of the conference center addition."

"Yes. He told you Paul was doing a great job."

"Right. And he handed you back the water glass, and you drank from that same glass," Chloe informed her.

"And *that* made you come to the conclusion that we were lovers? Because I drank from the same glass he did?" Madeline asked, astonished by her friend's logic.

Chloe grinned again, evidently quite pleased with her deductive abilities. "It's called intimacy, Maddie. It's something lovers do. They drink from the same glass. Eat from each other's plates. It's there between you and Chase."

So much for discretion, Madeline concluded, groaning. *How often had they done things just like that without conscious thought? And how many other people had noticed just as Chloe had?*

"Hey, it's nothing to be upset about," Chloe consolingly. "Personally, I think it's great. It's about time you settled down and got busy working on some little playmates for your goddaughter."

"Playmates? What are you talking about?"

Her friend gave her a puzzled frown. "Why I'm talking about you and Chase, of course. You know, the two of you getting married, starting a family."

"For heaven's sake, Chloe. This is the nineties. Just because two people are sleeping together doesn't mean they have to get married. Chase and I are having an affair. That's all."

Chloe leaned forward, her eyes dark, somber and filled with that disgusting knowledge that came with being a life-long friend who knew everything about you. "This may be the nineties, but you're still the same girl you've always been, Madeline Claire Charbonnet. You're the same girl who agonized over going to bed with Bradley and didn't, even when you were engaged to him, because you knew in your heart you didn't love him. If you're sleeping with Chase McAllister, it's because you're in love with him."

The words stung, bringing home the reality of the neat little corner she had painted herself into. She was in love with her lover, embroiled in an affair with a man who wanted her body, but not her heart. In love with a man who had made it clear at the outset that he wanted no strings and promised no future. "I am," Madeline admitted.

"So what's the problem?"

"I'm not sure how he feels about me. I know he wants me physically and he seems to care about me, but after the conference center addition is completed next month, he'll be going back to New Jersey."

"Has he said anything about the future?" Chloe asked.

"No. He's seemed on edge lately. At first I thought it was because of my father. The two of them really don't see eye to eye on things. But the last couple of times I tried to talk to him about the renovations nearing completion or the construction winding down, he cut me off. Last week when I asked when he thought he'd be leaving, he told me when his job was finished and stormed out of my place."

"Maybe it's because he doesn't want to go, but doesn't know how to tell you he wants to stay."

"You think so?" Madeline asked, hope fluttering anew inside her.

"I don't see why not. Have you told him how you feel? That you want him to stay?"

Madeline shook her head. "We agreed to an affair with no strings. That's why we've tried to be discreet. So there wouldn't be any explanations needed when things ended." Madeline paused. "But maybe it's time I let Chase know I've changed my mind."

"Thatta girl."

And she would start right now, Madeline decided smiling. Instead of dinner at some out of the way restaurant that ended back at her place this Friday, she would ask Chase to accompany her to the Wine Society's Annual Dinner. It would mark their first public appearance together as a couple. And when the evening was over and they returned to her house, she would confess she loved him.

Excitement bubbled inside her. Rising, Madeline went around the table and gave Chloe a hug. "Thanks a million, pal. I've got to run."

"But what about lunch? You're buying, remember?"

Madeline laughed. "Put it on my tab. There's a certain fellow that I've got to find and ask for a date."

Chase shifted the box of roses he was holding to his other arm and fished out the key that Madeline had given him to her house. He hesitated a moment, then slipped the key back into his pocket. Tonight was an official date, not a lovers' assignation. And it marked the first time they would venture out as a couple to an event where they would encounter Madeline's friends and peers. Satisfaction shot through him with the speed of a bullet at the unspoken declaration their arriving at the dinner together would make. It was chauvinistic, Chase admitted as he rang the doorbell, but he wanted every man there to know that she belonged to him.

As he waited for Madeline to respond, Chase pondered yet again what she was up to. Because she was up to something, he decided, recalling the glow in those expressive eyes when she had asked him to accompany her to the Wine Society's Annual Dinner. Would those eyes burn an even hotter green when he told her he had recommended her for the assistant GM position at the hotel?

"Chase." Madeline said his name with surprise as she opened the door to him. "Did you forget your key?" she asked, her voice a breathless whisper that put his body on immediate alert.

His heart stopped for a full beat. The excuse for a dress that she was wearing, a red slip of a thing held together with rhinestone straps and defining every one of her curves, turned up the heat. He eased a finger under the collar of his tux shirt and wished he could ease the tightness in his lower body as easily. "No," Chase nearly choked on the word. "I thought maybe you'd prefer not having me barge in on you tonight."

"I like it when you barge in on me." She kissed his mouth, a slow innocent brush of her lips that had desire licking through him like flames.

He had desired a woman before, Chase admitted, as he stepped inside and handed her the box of roses. No matter how intense, that desire had always been quickly sated and just as quickly forgotten. Except with Madeline. No matter how many times he made love to her, no matter how many times he quenched his insatiable thirst for her, it wasn't enough. He wanted her again. He wanted her now.

"Oh, Chase, they're lovely." The sweet scent swirled in the air, wrapping her in its sweetness, tangling him more deeply in her spell. Removing the long stems from the bed of tissue, Madeline lifted the red blooms to her face and breathed deeply.

Something curled inside Chase's chest as he watched her. He remembered the first time he had seen her and likened her to the expensive flower. She was beautiful, intoxicating, all velvet softness—just like the roses she held. He wanted to crush her to him, lose himself in that softness. And because he wanted it so badly, he refused to allow himself to touch her.

"Thank you," she whispered.

Chase took the mouth she offered, forcing himself to kiss her gently when he wanted to plunder, giving when he wanted to take. He didn't want to want her this badly. He hated feeling a victim to this need for her. When she pressed her hands against his chest and withdrew from the kiss, he released her. His heart hammered in his chest. His body trembled with need. She was every bit as exquisite as the roses she now fondled. And her effect on him was just as dangerous, just as deadly as the thorns that lined the stems of those beauties.

"I'd better put these in water and finish getting dressed," she murmured. "My father is expecting us."

The mention of Henri's name had the effect of a dousing in the Mississippi River, and it was even less appealing. He followed her into the kitchen and watched as she filled a vase with water. "I didn't realize we'd be seeing your father." Although he should have, Chase realized. From what Madeline had told him, the Wine Society was a group of elite individuals, primarily hoteliers and restaurateurs, who celebrated and shared their appreciation of fine wines.

"My father's been a member of the society for years. He never misses the dinner. He's reserved an entire table for tonight's affair. When I told him that we would be attending, he insisted we sit with him. You don't really mind, do you?"

He did mind, but it was too late to do anything about it. "Does he know you're coming with me?" Chase asked, unable to keep the defiant note out of his voice.

Madeline looked up from the flowers she had been arranging. "I told him you and I would be there together and that it wasn't business. He seemed fine about it, Chase. Really. Besides, he seemed preoccupied. I think he's got some sort of surprise planned. He said he had a special announcement to make at the dinner, and he wanted us both to be there."

A special announcement, Chase mused. He didn't like the sound of that. He didn't trust it, either. Had Charbonnet somehow managed to put together the money he would need to cover his share of the expenses for the conference center addition? Although he had been told up front when he had agreed to the expansion plans that, as part owner, he would need to come up with the money, the other man had seemed unconcerned. It certainly hadn't hampered his spending habits. And as far as Chase could tell, the fellow had continued to go through money at a rapid pace. While he might still have some of the proceeds left from his sale to Majestic, it wouldn't be enough.

Madeline chuckled as she inserted another stem. "Who knows with my father? Maybe they've elected him as the new president of the Wine Society. He would certainly love that. Whatever it is, he's excited about it. He was like a child on Christmas morning.''

Chase frowned. He had waited and worked too long to exact his revenge on Charbonnet to see it slip away now. Not when he was so close.

"What do you think?"

Chase pulled his thoughts back to the present. He looked at Madeline's face. Something twisted inside him at the look in her eyes. A man could search a lifetime and never have a woman look at him like that. With that mixture of affection and warmth, that kick of desire and greed.

"Chase?"

Suddenly he lost all enthusiasm for going to the dinner. He didn't want to think about her father, about his promise for revenge. He wanted to make love to Madeline, to soothe this insatiable craving to feel her beneath him. He wanted to free his body and soul of this . . . this need for her and to have her look at him that way a while longer.

"Beautiful," Chase finally managed to say. "They're almost as beautiful as you."

"My, you're quite the flatterer tonight, Mr. McAllister. Almost poetic. Must be the tux.''

Chase grinned at her teasing. "Could be. My guess is it's the woman. You inspire all sorts of things in me, Princess. The least of which is poetry.''

Her face heated, sending a delicate flush to her cheeks. "Well, why don't you work on the poetry while I finish getting dressed.''

"I have a better idea," Chase said, reaching for her. He tugged her against him and pressed his mouth to her neck. Her breath made that hitching sound, and desire whipped through him. He slid the rhinestone strap down one shoulder, traced the bare skin with his tongue. Madeline shivered. So did he. "What do you say I help you get undressed and then we spend the evening here?"

"That's a tempting offer," she whispered, her breath catching as he repeated the process to her other shoulder. "But we really do have to go. My father would be disappointed if we didn't show up. Remember, he said he had a surprise."

Henri Charbonnet had been full of surprises, Chase thought as he watched the other man laugh and play host to his elegant friends. Chase zeroed in on the face of the biggest and most unwelcome surprise of all—Bradley Eastman. Charming, good-looking and with a pedigree as long as his arm, Chase disliked everything about Madeline's ex-fiancé. He disliked even more the fact that Eastman's smarts and hotel-oriented background made him a perfect match for Madeline.

The object of his dislike leaned closer and whispered something to Madeline. When she tipped back her head in laughter, Chase wanted to smash the other man's face in the plate of trout Eugene.

"Chase, Henri tells me that you're going to be abandoning us and returning to New Jersey soon."

Chase jerked his attention to Bitsy Laurent—another of Henri's surprises that evening. The moment he had seen the newspaper's society editor he had wondered just what Henri's little announcement entailed, that he wanted press coverage.

"Is it true? Are you actually going to leave our fair city for the Northeast?"

"Everything has to come to an end sometime. As much as I like New Orleans, it's not my home." Chase reached for his wine, took a sip and immediately wished he could trade the expensive dry wine for the bite of whiskey.

"When will you be leaving?"

"In a few weeks. After the conference center addition is complete." And Henri Charbonnet was destroyed. For some reason the thought gave him no pleasure tonight. He should be happy it was nearly over. His revenge would be complete, and he could return home and get on with his life. Yet the thought of leaving depressed him.

"Wait until you see the conference center, Bitsy," Henri told her. "It's a marvelous piece of work. Not one of those cold glass-and-steel jobs. I insisted it be designed to blend in with the elegance and beauty of the Saint Charles.''

"Elegance and beauty aside," Bitsy began, swirling the wine in her glass. "The Saint Charles is not all that convenient to the convention trade. Do you really think you'll be able to sell it, Henri?"

"Madeline's already sold it," Chase informed her. "She has it booked solid for the months of September and October and most of November. As far as convenience, Madeline came up with the perfect solution. Free transportation to our guests on one of the city's landmarks—the street-cars."

"I'm impressed," Bitsy said. "Congratulations, Henri. You, too, Madeline. I guess the Saint Charles really is making a comeback."

Charbonnet beamed. "A big one."

Chase eyed his adversary, finding no enjoyment in knowing that when the conference center was complete, Charbonnet would be forced to relinquish another chunk of interest in his beloved hotel—and with it what remained of his control.

His gaze strayed to Madeline, and when she looked at him, there was a sadness there that her smile didn't disguise. The sick, churning feeling hit him again.

Guilt. It wrenched in his gut. She was going to hate him for hurting her father and for taking another piece of her hotel. Chase stamped down on the rush of emptiness that realization brought. It couldn't be helped. He had to do this for his mother. Besides, it was too late to stop things now. Everything was already in motion.

Charbonnet rose from his seat at the head of the table. He tapped his fork against the stem of his wineglass and Chase, along with the other eight people at the table, turned their attention to him. "Friends. Friends. I was going to save my announcement until after dessert, but now that Bitsy has brought up the subject of the Saint Charles and the conference center addition, I think now might be the appropriate time to tell you about another addition that is about to take place. As most of you know, the new conference center and renovation have been taking up a lot of my time. So has the increase in business. It doesn't leave many hours for me to be with my friends."

Chase tensed, but he managed a smile while the others at the table laughed at Henri's joke.

"At any rate, managing the Saint Charles has become quite a demanding job. One I love, but don't want to handle alone anymore. My partners at Majestic Hotels agree with me, and we've decided to appoint an assistant general manager."

Chase frowned. Something was wrong. He could feel it in his bones. Charbonnet had fought him bitterly over the creation of the Assistant GM position and had lost the battle. He'd submitted no names for consideration for the vote that was scheduled to take place at the board meeting next week. In fact, Chase's own letter recommending Madeline had been sent that very morning in the express pouch, along with the monthly reports.

"My friends, I'd like to present the new assistant general manager of the Saint Charles Hotel and the young man that I hope will someday be my son-in-law and take over the reins of my family's legacy. Bradley Eastman."

Stunned, Chase darted his gaze across the table to Madeline. The burst of jealousy died instantly. The phony smile was pasted on her lips, but her skin was the color of chalk. Her eyes were the deep green of the Caribbean Sea at dawn and held a wealth of pain.

Chase set down his wineglass before he snapped the stem. "You're being a little premature with your announcements, Charbonnet. Both of them," he told Henri, not bothering to keep the edge out of his voice. The loud chatter at the table dimmed, but he didn't care. "The board doesn't vote on that position until next week."

Henri smiled at him. "I spoke to Jamison and the others this afternoon. Faxed them a copy of Bradley's résumé. They were quite impressed. And since you hadn't made any recommendation, they agreed to go with mine. Bradley's approval will simply be a matter of formality and handled at the meeting next week."

"I'm afraid it won't be quite that simple," Chase told him through gritted teeth. "I've recommended Madeline for the job, and I intend to see that she gets it."

"Madeline?" Charbonnet repeated.

"Yes, you know. Your daughter. The one who runs the hotel half the time so you can attend little society parties like this one."

"Chase. Father, please. I appreciate your vote of confidence, Chase, but my father's made his recommendation and I . . . I think Bradley's an excellent choice. Congratulations, Bradley. I wish you the best." She lifted her glass and proposed a toast to the other man.

Chase didn't even pretend to drink. He simply stared at her, pain ripping through him for her. He wanted to strangle the old man for hurting her. And himself for adding to her hurt by stalling over his recommendation while he toyed with her father in a power play. Guilt and anger dealt alternating blows to his solar plexus. He deserved every one of them.

Madeline's cheeks ached at the effort it took to keep smiling when all she wanted to do was bawl. She didn't know which was worse, she decided, as dessert was served. Watching Chase beat himself up or witnessing her father's dismay. Of course, it didn't help that her spirits were already dragging like an anchor, at Chase's mention of returning to New Jersey. Her father's surprise had only condemned them to the darkest pits.

"Madeline, your father said you weren't interested in the job," Bradley told her, worry marring his handsome face. "If he was wrong about that . . . and about us—"

"We'll talk about it later," Madeline told him. Her father had been wrong on both counts. She *had* wanted the job—desperately. But more than the job, she had wanted her father's vote of confidence. She hadn't gotten it. And she wouldn't be able to give him Bradley Eastman as a son-in-law, either—not when she was in love with Chase.

But she would deal with her father later. Not now. The hurt and anger were still too raw. The one thing tonight's little fiasco had accomplished was to bring home the futility of ever winning his approval. It had also brought home the futility of the game she had been playing with Chase.

Everything has to end sometime. Chase's words played over and over in her head and had hurt far more than her father's rejection. She had agreed to Chase's plan—sex with no strings attached—and had changed the rules mid-stream by falling in love with him. It wasn't his fault, but in that moment she almost hated him for it. Well, her pride had taken a big enough battering for one night. She would not subject it to more by begging Chase not to leave. Pain bubbled inside her and she blinked back the tears.

Darn it. I am not going to cry. That was one more thing she could blame Chase for, she decided, fanning anger to blot out the pain. She had never been a weepy female—not before she had met him.

Bradley asked her a question. Her father said something to her. She fumbled with answers, her eyes on Chase. He simply stared at her, his expression cold and unyielding. *Everything has to end sometime.*

She had to get out of here. Away from her father. Away from Chase. "I have a monster headache," she announced, coming to her feet. "Please excuse me."

"Madeline, dear. Are you all right?"

"Madeline!"

She heard her father and Chase call out her name. She hurried across the dining room and raced out to the street. "Could you get me a taxi, please?" she asked the doorman.

The man let out a shrill whistle, and a yellow cab pulled up to the curb. He opened the door, and she started to slide onto the back seat.

Chase grabbed her arm. "Just where the hell do you think you're going?"

"Home." She attempted to shake off his viselike grip.

"Not without me, you're not."

"Go back to the dinner party, Chase. I want to be alone."

"Tough. You've got company." He slammed the door shut to the cab and marched her over to his car which the valet had left running.

"Ma'am, if the gentleman is bothering you—"

"Beat it," Chase growled at the doorman, and the elderly man retreated. He jerked open the door. "Get in, Madeline. Whether you like it or not, I'm taking you home."

Madeline met that cold, hard gaze for a moment, then whipped around and got into the car. The drive was made in heavy silence. When they pulled up in front of her house, she didn't waste her breath telling him not to come in.

He went straight to the bar and poured her a snifter of brandy. He led her to the couch and ordered her to sit. "Here. Drink this."

"I'm not thirsty."

He grabbed her hand and shoved the glass in it. "Drink it anyway. You've had a shock. Hell, I've had a shock. And I'm not even in love with that old place the way you are." He dragged his hands through his hair as he paced back and forth like a caged tiger. "I know you're angry and you're hurting, Princess."

She was angry and she was hurting. But it wasn't only her father's shot to her confidence that was causing that anger and pain. It was Chase. Knowing that he didn't love her. Knowing that he would soon be gone. She sipped the brandy, let it burn a path down her throat and settle in a pool of heat in her stomach.

Chase sat down beside her. He removed the empty glass from her fingers, placed it on the table, then took both of her hands in his. "I'm sorry about what happened. It's as much my fault as your father's that this happened tonight. But I don't want you to worry. I'm going to call Jamison at home in the morning. The assistant GM job is yours."

"I don't care about the job, Chase. Bradley can have it."

"I don't believe you. I know how much that hotel means to you."

Madeline could see his mouth move, but all she could hear were the words he'd said at the table. *Everything has to end sometime.*

One last time, she told herself. She would love him one last time, feel his arms around her, the weight of his body as they became one. One more memory to last her a lifetime, and then she would let go.

"Don't clam up on me like this, Princess." Chase grabbed her shoulders and gave her a gentle shake. "Talk to me."

"I don't want to talk anymore," she murmured, stripping away his tie and unfastening his shirt with a skill she hadn't known she possessed. She felt his body tense, when she pressed her mouth to his chest.

"This isn't the answer," he told her, his breath catching as her tongue circled his flat nipple.

"I'm not asking you for answers. That's not what our relationship is about. You're not my confidant, Chase. You're not even my friend. That's not what I want from you."

Chase caught her chin and forced her to look into his eyes. "Tell me what you think our relationship is about, Madeline. What is it you want from me?"

Madeline hesitated. There was anger in his eyes, dark and forbidding. Was he mad because he'd discovered she'd been stupid enough to fall in love with him? Did he think she would demand more than he'd offered? More than they had agreed on? Her pride wouldn't let her. With a brazenness spurred by that pride, she sat on her knees and pulled the red dress up and over her head. She tossed it onto the floor. Unhooking the strapless lace, covering her breasts, she pitched it next to the dress. "Sex, Chase. That's what this affair has been all about from the start. And that's what I want from you."

His nostrils flared. A muscle ticked in his cheek. Fury. She could feel it. Smell it clash with the scent of the roses he'd given her earlier. His eyes raked over her bare breasts, searing her with just a look, making her body burn without even touching her. When he lifted his gaze to hers, Madeline's pulse jumped as she watched the fury mingle with a different kind of heat.

Her heart hammered in her chest, and she considered telling him the truth. That she loved him. That she didn't want him to leave. But then Chase was stripping off his slacks, reaching for her, guiding her on to the source of his heat.

And then there was no more room for words, no more room for wondering if she had made a mistake by not confessing the truth. There was only room for feeling as their bodies moved together in a frenzied race toward the raging blaze, until they cried out and tumbled into the flames.

Moments later Chase eased himself from her. Immediately Madeline missed his weight and warmth. She stretched out her fingers and stroked his back. He stiffened beneath her touch. Standing, he reached for his slacks.

"Where are you going?"

"Back to the hotel."

"Chase, about what I said earlier. I want to explain."

He zipped up his pants and dragged on his shirt. "Oh, I don't think you need to explain anything, Princess. You made yourself perfectly clear."

He shoved his feet into his shoes and crammed his tie into his pocket. When he turned back around to face her, there was anger and hurt in his eyes. "You know how to reach me. The next time you want stud service, just give me a call."

Twelve

She had hurt him. Madeline realized that now as she hung up the phone and pulled out her overnight bag. In her jumbled emotional state she had lashed out at Chase, batted away his offer and need to comfort. Worst of all, in her despair over loving him and not having his love in return, she had demeaned what they did share by equating it to animal lust. It didn't matter that it was a lie. The damage had been done. She had hurt him.

Madeline sighed, remembering the look on Chase's face before he'd left her. Anger had shimmered in those blue eyes. And revulsion. For himself or for her she wasn't sure. Probably both. But even greater than the anger and disgust, there had been pain. So much pain . . . Madeline swallowed and pressed her fingers to her chest as the tightening sensation gripped her again, like a vise squeezing her heart.

It was amazing, she thought, the difference a week could make. The few days' leave she had taken from the hotel had helped. It had enabled her to put her life into perspective. Her dogged determination to prove herself to her father had consumed too much of her life. Their heart-to-heart talk had been long overdue. She had forgiven him. How could she not when it was his love for her that made him want more for her than the demanding life of a hotelier? At least now he had accepted that a career in hotels was what she wanted. But it was no longer the only thing she wanted. She wanted Chase. The question was did Chase want her? Would he forgive her and give their relationship a chance?

Stepping over to her dressing table, Madeline unzipped her cosmetic bag and dropped in lipsticks, powders and pencils. There was only one way to find out. She'd start by telling Chase the truth—that she loved him. Her stomach fluttered. For the hundredth time in the past week, Madeline prayed that she wasn't making a mistake by thinking that Chase cared about her, too.

And if he doesn't? What have I lost? Besides her pride, nothing. And if she was right... Madeline smiled and pulled the zipper closed on the case. If she was right, she would have Chase's love.

Her optimism returning, Madeline retrieved her toothbrush from the bathroom and dumped it along with the cosmetics bag into her suitcase. She tucked in a bottle of French perfume.

She was probably crazy, Madeline told herself. Life with a man like Chase would never be easy. He was a shade too handsome, definitely arrogant and far too sure of himself. Of course, he was also kind, generous to a fault and had a body that made even a Southern lady break out in a sweat.

Holding up the wispy nightgown she'd ransomed from the window of a French Quarter lingerie shop, Madeline grinned and folded it in the suitcase. No, life with Chase would never be easy, but it also wouldn't be dull.

After snapping the locks on her suitcase, she reached for the telephone, punched out the number for the Saint Charles Hotel and asked for room service. "Hi, this is Madeline Charbonnet. I'd like to order room service for Mr. Mc-Allister's suite. He'll be returning to the hotel late this evening, and I'd like to have a light supper for two waiting. I'd like to begin with a bottle of champagne. Moët & Chandon 1976..."

Chase removed his briefcase and travel bag from the trunk of his car and slammed it shut. Bone tired from an endless round of meetings and the late-evening flight, he walked across the dark hotel garage, the sound of his leather soles slapping against the pavement. He stepped out onto the sidewalk. The heat and hundred-degree humidity smacked him in the face. Even at night, Chase thought, as he shifted his briefcase under his arm to loosen his tie, August in New Orleans was almost intolerable.

So why did returning here tonight feel like coming home? And why now, when his revenge against Henri Charbonnet was less than twenty-four hours away, did he feel no sense of triumph? Why instead of happiness did he feel such an emptiness inside?

He already knew the answer—Madeline. Sighing, Chase nodded to the hotel doorman as he walked into the lobby and pushed the signal button for the elevator. She was the reason the prospect of waiting for an easier morning flight had held no appeal. She was the reason the revenge he had hungered for so long and now had within his reach brought him no satisfaction.

The doors to the elevator whooshed open and he stepped inside. After pressing his floor number, he leaned against the wall and closed his eyes. It was a mistake. Because the moment his eyes shut, Madeline was there again. Not that that was a surprise. He had seen her face repeatedly during the past week. When he was negotiating his deal with Majestic for a larger interest in the Saint Charles. When he had tried without success to sleep. He had seen her expressive eyes bright and shining with laughter at the Jazzfest, filled with passion and wonder as they made love, with pain and hurt at her father's rejection. But most of all he remembered that tangle of passion and anger that had shimmered in their depths the last time they'd been together, when she had told him she wanted the passion he brought to her bed and nothing more.

Her words had angered him. Her touch had fueled his desire. And when it was over, he'd been left with nothing but that sick, empty feeling. That same feeling he had now. He'd told her he wanted sex with no strings, and she'd given it to him. Only afterward he'd realized it wasn't what he wanted at all. He wanted Madeline's love.

And after tomorrow, he would have only her hate.

The elevator dinged, announcing his floor. Chase wiped his hand over his face. Picking up his bags, he stepped out into the hall and headed for his suite. He would call her tonight, ask to see her and tell her the truth before her father received the papers in the morning. She would still hate him. There was no chance she wouldn't. She loved her father and the hotel too much not to hate him for what he'd done. That he hadn't wanted to hurt her wouldn't matter.

He slipped the key into the lock and pushed open the door. Chase frowned as the strains of Tchaikovsky floated in the air. Dropping his bags to the floor, he pushed the door closed behind him and moved into the room. Slender tapers burned from polished candlesticks on the antique dining table, where fine china and crystal had been set for two. A bottle of champagne sat majestically in an ice bucket. Tiny beads of moisture inched slowly down the sides of the gleaming silver receptacle like tears down a woman's face. Chase walked over and pulled out the bottle to inspect the label.

"I hope you approve of the champagne."

Chase jerked his gaze upward at the sound of Madeline's voice. His breath caught in his throat. He forgot how to breathe. She stood in the doorway of the bedroom with her hair flowing about her shoulders, her eyes shining like gems, her mouth painted a dangerous red. And she was wearing some wispy white thing designed for sin.

"I believe '76 was a good year for that particular brand. Is it okay?"

Chase nodded, not trusting that he could actually speak. He heard the whisper of silk against her skin as she walked toward him. The faint rose scent that always seemed a part of her curled itself around him, clouding his senses. Then she was standing in front of him, the candlelight at her back, outlining the curve of her breasts, the line of her hips. His gaze drifted lower where he could see the shadow at the top of her thighs. Chase swallowed and squeezed the neck of the champagne.

Madeline looked down at his fingers clutching the bottle in his fist and then shifted her gaze back up to his face. Mischief gleamed in her eyes. The hint of a smile curved her lips. "Were you planning to open that or just strangle it?"

Chase blinked. He glanced at the bottle clenched in his fist and eased his grip. "That depends on the reason both you and the champagne are here."

"To make a confession." She stepped closer, her body a mere breath away, her face lifted to his. Her hands cupped the sides of his face. "To ask you to forgive me. I lied to you, Chase."

"Madeline, don't. It's not necessary." He felt like a snake. It was he who had sins that needed confessing. He who had lied through omission. He who was in need of her forgiveness. He would tell her the truth now and pray that somehow she would forgive him, that they would still have a chance. "I'm the one who needs to ask forgiveness. I—"

She pressed her fingers to his mouth, silencing him. "That last time we were together when I told you that all I wanted from you was sex. That that was all there was between us. It wasn't true."

Chase caught her wrists. "Madeline, I—"

"I love you, Chase. I love you and I'm hoping I'm not wrong in thinking that you—" She swallowed. Her tongue flicked across her bottom lip and he could see the fear and vulnerability in her eyes. "—in thinking that you care for me, too."

"You're not wrong," he said, wrapping her in his arms as joy filled his heart. "Because I love you." He needed to tell her the truth now, all of it, he told himself as she kissed him. His only hope was that she would forgive him. Fear that she wouldn't warred with the new happiness inside him. Chase eased his mouth free to look at her face and try to explain. "Madeline, I love you."

"Show me, love." She slid her hand between them, cupped him and squeezed. "Show me."

Desire raced through him, a fever in his blood, a hungry beast demanding to be fed. He lifted her into his arms and carried her into the bedroom. First, he needed to tell her. First, he had to explain. He struggled, trying to find the right words. But then she was kissing him again, her hands tugging off his clothes, her fingers stroking his hardness as she urged him to join her in the bed.

And then he couldn't speak. He couldn't think. All he could do was feel.

Her fingers felt like cool silk as she curled them around him, sending desire and heat streaking through him again. Chase groaned. Not yet, he told himself, and captured her hands to end the pleasure and torture. First, he needed to show her how he felt, how much he loved her. How much he needed her in his life.

Stretching her arms over her head, he pulled the wisp of silk free from her body and tossed it to the floor. His breath quickened as he feasted on the sight of her naked flesh. "You look like a pagan goddess," he whispered, and need licked through him as her eyes darkened with desire. "My pagan goddess."

Still holding her wrists captive, he lowered his mouth to her breasts, swirling his tongue around the tip of first one and then the other.

"Chase!" She struggled, trying to free her wrists from the prison of his fingers.

"Not yet," he murmured, closing his teeth over the darkened nipple before drawing it into his mouth. He paid homage to her other breast, then slowly shifted his mouth to kiss the tender flesh at her rib cage, down her stomach. Using his free hand, Chase ripped away the scrap of lace and tangled his fingers in the nest of curls between her thighs.

Madeline whimpered. She struggled for freedom and he released her hands. Her fingers clutched at him. "Please, Chase. I need you inside me."

"And I want to be there. But first, let me love you," he whispered, fighting his own need to join their bodies. He wanted to give to her, to show her how much she had given him.

Opening the tender folds that hid the sensitive bud of her womanhood, he lowered his head.

Madeline gripped the wrought iron rail at the head of the bed. She arched her body, crying out his name as the first spasms hit her.

A shudder went through him at her response. He continued to love her with his mouth, his excitement growing each time her body quivered beneath the stroke of his tongue. He flicked his tongue across the sensitive nub once more, while easing a finger inside her honeyed warmth.

Madeline cried out. And then her hands were reaching for him again, grabbing his hair and dragging his mouth to hers. "I love you," she whispered before guiding him into her warmth.

"Madeline!" Chase sheathed himself in her, surrounding himself with her love.

Somehow, he promised himself as he drove them both towards that bright ball of red fire. Somehow, he would find a way to keep her love—because without it he wasn't sure he could survive.

Madeline opened her eyes as the fingers of dawn spilled through the window. Smiling, she brushed the hair back from Chase's forehead and caressed the stubble of whiskers that shadowed his cheek. Her body would bear the marks of those whiskers, she thought, recalling the number of times they'd made love during the night and into the early morning hours. But she had no regrets. How could she, when there had been such an intensity to Chase's lovemaking, so much emotion in his declaration that they would sit down and discuss the future this morning?

The future. That they would have one together, she no longer doubted. She smiled again, warmed by the thought, and allowed her fingertips to drift over the scar on his chin.

Chase captured her fingers and brought them to his lips. "Good morning," he told her, pulling her over on top of him. He drew her head down and kissed her.

"Morning," she murmured when he released her mouth. "Do you want the bathroom first? I put out the card on the door last night for room service. It'll be here soon."

His hands stilled on her hips. The laughter disappeared from his eyes. "We need to talk, Madeline. There's something I need to tell you."

Uneasiness whispered along her spine. "All right. Why don't we—" A series of raps sounded at the door. "That must be room service," she said strangely relieved by the interruption.

"I'll get it," he told her. "You go ahead and get dressed. I'll meet you in the other room."

Chase watched as Madeline walked away and closed the bathroom door behind her. Shoveling his hands through his hair, he prayed somehow he'd find the right words to make her understand. He didn't want to lose her. Not now. Not when he'd just realized how much she meant to him.

The pounding started at the door again. Frowning, Chase pulled on his slacks and went to the other room. Ready to take a bite out of the room-service waiter, he jerked open the door.

"You bastard." Henri Charbonnet stormed in, his face red with anger, his eyes narrowed slits, a legal-looking document curled in his fist. "You stole my hotel from me."

"I didn't steal anything, Charbonnet," Chase said, pulling up the zipper on his fly. He walked over to the mini refrigerator and pulled out a container of juice. "You lost it all by yourself. I warned you that you'd have to come up with your share of the money for the overruns on the renovations and the conference center addition... use some of the money you got from Majestic for their interest in the hotel."

"I don't have enough, and you know it."

Chase pulled back the seal on the orange juice and drank it straight from the plastic bottle. Setting the juice down, he wiped his hand across his mouth. "You can always ask Majestic for an advance against future profits."

"You already know they turned me down. Thanks to you." Charbonnet stalked over to him, hatred in his eyes.

"You can quit the cat-and-mouse game, McAllister. I talked to Jamison this morning. I know you're one of Majestic's partners and I know all about the deal you cut with them giving *you* the interest in my hotel. He faxed me a copy of the demand letter that's being delivered today." Raising the crumpled document in his fist, he threw it at Chase. It hit him in the chest and fell to the floor.

"You might have succeeded in stealing the Saint Charles from me, but you're not going to steal my daughter. Madeline's convinced herself she's in love with you, but she won't be when I tell her what you've done. She'll wash her hands of you like that." He snapped his fingers. "And I for one will be glad. You're scum, McAllister," he said, his lips curling. "You're not fit to breathe the same air with her."

Angered, Chase gave him a thin smile. "I've got news for you, Madeline and I have shared a lot more than just air."

Charbonnet stiffened. He ran a glance over Chase's half-dressed state, and then his eyes darted to the closed bedroom door. "Why you lousy—" He lunged at Chase.

Chase blocked the blow and pinned the older man to the wall, his arm pressed across his windpipe.

"Keep away from my daughter."

"Why? Don't think I'm good enough for her?" Years of rage and hatred, of grief for a mother he had lost too soon, for family holidays he had never known, for the familial love that had never been there, churned inside Chase. He stared at the man responsible for it all. He wanted to hurt him as he had been hurt. "Is that it? You think I'm not good enough for Madeline the same way my mother wasn't good enough for you?"

"What are you talking about?" Charbonnet pushed at the arm blocking his throat. "I don't even know your mother."

"Oh, but you did know her at one time. Quite well, in fact. Her name was Katie...Katie McAllister. Twenty-six years ago she worked for you as a waitress right here in this hotel. She was also your mistress."

"No," he whispered, his face paling. His body started to tremble. "It's not true."

"Don't lie to me. I know it was you. I heard her on the phone with you that day—she called you by name." The scene came back to Chase, spinning him back to the past and the painful sight of his beautiful mother weeping. "She told you she loved you, pleaded with you not to end the affair, to let her come to the hotel to see you. You hung up on her. When she called you back, told you she loved you, begged you to forget about the hotel and go away with her, you hung up on her again. And then you refused the rest of her calls."

"You're mistaken."

"No, I'm not. I heard everything. I was home from school that day because I'd fallen and split open my chin."

Madeline stood frozen in the doorway. Her breath lodged in her throat as she watched her father's eyes drop to Chase's chin. Could it be true? Had her father and Chase's mother been lovers?

"You wanted revenge," her father accused.

"Yes."

Revenge. Had that been what Chase had wanted all along? Had that been the reason he had set out to seduce her? To avenge her father's sin against his mother? Pain sliced through her. She wrapped her arms around herself, feeling as though she would rip in two.

"Did you even care when you found out that she'd put a gun to her head and pulled the trigger that night?" Chase grabbed her father by his jacket and shook him. "Did you?" he demanded.

"Stop it!"

Chase whirled around. Seeing her, he released her father and started toward her. "Madeline, I can explain."

"No! Stay back." She rubbed her arms, trying to stop the trembling and the awful pain inside her. *Oh, God, it hurts. It hurts so bad.* "How could I have been so stupid? I believed you loved me, but you were only using me. You used me to hurt my father. And I made it so easy by falling in love with you." She laughed, the sound as hollow as the feeling inside her.

"You're wrong, Madeline. Please believe me, you're wrong. I admit I did want revenge against your father. That's why I had Majestic buy into the hotel . . . to take it away from him. The way he had taken my mother away from me. But you . . ." His voice broke. "You were never a part of that plan. I fell in love with you. I'm still in love with you."

He started toward her again, and she cried out, "No! Don't come near me. Don't touch me." Madeline shuddered. "I couldn't bear to have you ever touch me again."

Chase jerked back as though she had hit him. She forced herself to look away, not wanting to fool herself into believing it was pain she saw in his eyes at her rejection. Afraid because she wanted to believe him so badly that she would. Blinking back tears, she shifted her gaze to her father. He lay slumped on the floor, clutching his chest. "Father!" She raced to his side. "Father, what's wrong?"

"Pain," he whispered. "Bad pain in my chest."

Chase took her by the shoulders and moved her aside. Then he was easing her father's head to the floor, checking his pulse, listening to his heart. Another pain gripped him. "Call 911, Madeline. Now! I think he's having a heart attack."

The ten minutes seemed like an eternity. But as the paramedics placed her father onto the stretcher, he refused to leave until Madeline let him speak to Chase. "You got it all wrong, McAllister," he whispered. "It wasn't me."

Madeline squeezed his hand. "Father, please."

"No. He needs to know the truth. It wasn't me with your mother. It was my father."

"She called you by name. You came to the funeral."

He coughed and clutched his chest again. "My father and I had the same name. I went to the funeral to spare my mother. She'd found out about Katie. My father confessed, and he asked her for a divorce. She refused and threatened to take away the hotel. That's why he broke it off. It wasn't me. For me there was never anyone but my Lillie. Ask Madeline."

"It's true," Madeline told him. "My parents were very much in love. It nearly killed my father when she died."

Shock. Disbelief. Resignation that he had been wrong. Madeline saw all of it register on Chase's face. He looked so lost, so alone. She remembered the stories Chase had told her of his childhood, and because she hadn't learned yet how not to love him, a part of her wanted to reach out and comfort him. She squashed the notion and hardened her heart. "You got your revenge, Chase. I hope you find it sweet." Turning away, she followed the stretcher out of the room.

Revenge wasn't sweet, Chase thought as he waited for the call to come. It brought him no peace, no happiness. How could it, when the hate that had sustained his need for revenge had turned out to be a lie? When it had nearly cost an innocent man his life? When it had cost him the only woman he would ever love?

The phone jangled and Chase snatched it up on the first ring. "McAllister."

"Mr. McAllister, this is the front desk. Ms. Charbonnet just came into the hotel and she's getting on the elevator now."

"Thanks," Chase told the clerk. After replacing the receiver on the phone, he closed the door to his suite and started for the elevator at the end of the hall.

In the four weeks since Henri's release from the hospital, he had had time to do lots of soul searching. At last he had accepted that his mother had been responsible for making the decision to choose death over life without the man she loved. In doing so it had been his mother who had decided to abandon him. He had accepted it and forgiven her, although he would never understand her decision. Perhaps his mother had been too weak to fight; so had Madeline's grandfather, obviously.

He wasn't. Stepping onto the elevator, Chase punched out the floor number for Madeline's office. He loved Madeline, and despite her refusal to see or speak to him, he believed she still loved him. He hoped he wasn't wrong, Chase told himself as he exited the elevator and strode down the hall to her office. Because against everyone's advice he had risked everything he owned on a gamble that she did love him enough to forgive him. If he was wrong, then he had given her the instruments for her to seek her own revenge against him—the hotel and his heart.

"I see you got my letter," Chase told her.

Madeline's head jerked up, and she glared at him from her position on the floor. "I got your attorney's letter demanding that I clear my personal things from the office," she informed him. She dumped the contents of her bottom desk drawer into the cardboard box.

"That's right. You returned the letters I sent to you unopened. You refused my calls, too." Chase picked up one of the boxes and walked over to the bookshelves. "Want me to pack these for you?"

Her back stiffened, and the air in the room dropped another ten degrees. She shrugged. "Suit yourself. You could have saved yourself the legal fees, if you had just had my things packed up and sent to me the way I asked you to in my letter of resignation."

"I suppose I could have, but then I wouldn't have had a chance to see you again and tell you how sorry I am. I blame myself for your father's heart attack."

Madeline paused. "I know you do. And...well, you shouldn't. It was a minor attack, Chase. The stress of your fight with him probably didn't help, but apparently he was having problems for a long time. He's doing fine now. He just needs to watch his diet and keep his blood pressure under control."

Something softened in her eyes. "I appreciate you creating that ambassador position for him here at the hotel. I don't know if he'll actually take you up on it, but I think he was pleased by the offer."

"I hope Henri does decide to take it for the hotel's sake. He may not have been the best director I've ever worked with, but he was great at hotel relations. Besides, he still owns a third of the hotel." Chase took a plant from a top shelf. "Should I pack this?"

"Just put it on top of one of the boxes."

They worked in silence for the next ten minutes. When Madeline packed the last of the items from the top of her desk, Chase handed her the lid to the carton. "Looks like that's it," he said, giving the office a quick glance.

"Yes," she said, her voice little more than a whisper. Chase's chest tightened at the sad look in her eyes.

"Well, I'll just load these in my car and be out of your way." She picked up a box and walked to the door.

Chase blocked her path. "I'll have one of the bellmen carry them down for you."

"That's not necessary," Madeline told him. She needed to get out of here before she started crying, before she found herself begging him to hold her and tell her that he still loved her, that it all hadn't been a lie.

"I insist." He removed the box from her hands.

After the bellman had arrived with a small dolly and had loaded the boxes and plants, Chase said, "You can take it all to the executive floor and put them in the general manager's office."

"What? Those are my personal belongings. They don't belong to the hotel or to you. You tell him to come back here with my things right now."

She started after the bellman, who was already pushing the dolly onto the service elevator. Chase grabbed her arm and steered her to the main elevator. "Where do you think you're taking me?" she demanded, trying to pull free of his grasp and not succeeding.

"To the office of the new general manager of the Saint Charles."

"Chase, I do not want to go to your office. I have nothing more to say to you."

"Then you can listen, because there's quite a lot I have to say to you." He tipped her chin up and brushed his lips across hers. A quiver of longing raced over her skin, and Madeline cursed her traitorous body.

The doors to the elevator opened, and Chase marched her down the hall of the executive floor. "Why are you doing this, Chase? You've avenged your mother. You now control the hotel. You've gotten what you wanted."

They stopped in front of the office door, and Chase turned her to face him. "You're wrong. I don't have what I want, Madeline, not if I don't have you. I love you. Without you, the rest means nothing to me."

Her heart jumped to her throat, but before she could say anything, Chase was opening the door and urging her inside the office.

Roses. There were red roses everywhere. Hundreds of them spilling from crystal vases, painted wicker baskets, Waterford pitchers. They stood majestically, their petals looking like velvet, atop the antique desk, the credenza, the bookcases, even along the windowsill. They seemed to cover every inch of the room. She could barely make out the surface of the Queen Anne table or the new pearl carpet that covered the floor. Their perfumed scent filled the air with its sweetness.

"I had new wall coverings, drapes and carpets put in, but if you don't like them, you can redo it however you want."

Madeline blinked and noted for the first time the damask drapes of soft green, the mint and cream wall covering with just a hint of pale rose running through it. She turned to look at Chase. "I thought this was the new GM's office."

"It is," he said, smiling. "It's your office, Princess. You're the new GM of the Saint Charles."

"Me? But I resigned as sales director. You can't just appoint me as the general manager."

"I didn't appoint you. You inherited the job as majority owner of the Saint Charles." Chase took her hands, and Madeline realized that his were shaking. "It's yours now, Princess. Or at least the two-thirds that I bought from Majestic. I had it signed over to you."

"Why?" she asked, stunned.

"Because I love you, and I knew how much you loved this hotel. Even if you don't love me anymore and can't forgive me for what I've done, I couldn't keep the hotel. It's a part of you and should have been yours. Now it is."

"You can't do that. You can't just give me the hotel."

"Too late. I already did. The papers transferring my ownership to you are in an envelope over there on your desk. The Saint Charles is yours now."

Madeline whipped her gaze to where a fat legal envelope rested between two vases of the roses and then back to Chase. "But what will you do? I mean, you don't have a job anymore with Majestic. My father said you gave up your interest in the partnership and the other properties it owns in exchange for the Saint Charles."

Chase shrugged. "I've been thinking about opening up a hotel consulting firm. There are a lot of hotels in New Orleans. I might be able to offer them the benefit of my experience with Majestic."

Hope bloomed inside her. "You mean you would stay here? Not go back to New Jersey?"

"That's right. I thought I'd stick around and see if I could convince you to let me fill the job of being your lover, maybe try to work my way up to the position of husband."

He gave her that wicked grin, and Madeline's heart began to stammer. Chase loved her. The knowledge washed over her, filling her with joy.

"What do you say? Any chance of you giving me the job? I know a lot about the inner workings of hotels."

Madeline gave him a once-over. "I don't know," she said soberly and ruined it by grinning. "The hotel business is a crazy way of life. You'd have to put in lots of long, crazy hours. It would mean lots of overtime and you'd have to be willing to work nights."

"I don't mind," he told her, tugging her into his arms. He smiled at her. Devilment gleamed in his eyes. "I do some of my best work at night."

And then his mouth was on hers, kissing her, loving her, showing her how much she meant to him, because he didn't think he could find the words to tell her. When he lifted his head, Chase stared into those wondrous green eyes.

"You're hired," she whispered and dragged his mouth back to hers. And as she opened to him, the years of loneliness, the weeks of loving her and believing she was lost to him were over. At long last he was home.

*   *   *   *   *

A Funny Thing Happened on the Way to the Baby Shower...

When four college friends reunite to celebrate the arrival of one bouncing baby, they find four would-be grooms on the way!

Don't miss a single, sexy tale in

RAYE MORGAN'S

Only in

BABY DREAMS
in May '96 (SD #997)

A GIFT FOR BABY
in July '96 (SD #1010)

BABIES BY THE BUSLOAD
in September '96 (SD #1022)
And look for

INSTANT DAD, WILL TRAIN
in November '96
Only from

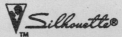

MILLION DOLLAR SWEEPSTAKES
AND EXTRA BONUS PRIZE DRAWING

SWP-ME96

As seen on TV!
Free Gift Offer

With a Free Gift proof-of-purchase from any Silhouette® book,
you can receive a beautiful cubic zirconia pendant.

This gorgeous marquise-shaped stone is a genuine cubic
zirconia—accented by an 18" gold tone necklace.

(Approximate retail value $19.95)

Send for yours today...
compliments of ▼ *Silhouette*®
™

To receive your free gift, a cubic zirconia pendant, send us one original proof-of-purchase, photocopies not accepted, from the back of any Silhouette Romance™, Silhouette Desire®, Silhouette Special Edition®, Silhouette Intimate Moments® or Silhouette Yours Truly™ title available in August, September or October at your favorite retail outlet, together with the Free Gift Certificate, plus a check or money order for $1.65 U.S./$2.15 CAN. (do not send cash) to cover postage and handling, payable to Silhouette Free Gift Offer. We will send you the specified gift. Allow 6 to 8 weeks for delivery. Offer good until October 31, 1996 or while quantities last. Offer valid in the U.S. and Canada only.

Free Gift Certificate

Name: _____

Address: _____

City: _____ State/Province: _____ Zip/Postal Code: _____

Mail this certificate, one proof-of-purchase and a check or money order for postage and handling to: SILHOUETTE FREE GIFT OFFER 1996. In the U.S.: 3010 Walden Avenue, P.O. Box 9077, Buffalo NY 14269-9077. In Canada: P.O. Box 613, Fort Erie, Ontario L2Z 5X3.

FREE GIFT OFFER   084-KMD
ONE PROOF-OF-PURCHASE
To collect your fabulous FREE GIFT, a cubic zirconia pendant, you must include this
original proof-of-purchase for each gift with the properly completed Free Gift Certificate.

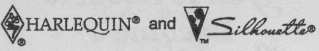

HARLEQUIN® and **Silhouette®**

are proud to present...

HERE COME THE
GROOMS™

Four marriage-minded stories written by top
Harlequin and Silhouette authors!

Next month, you'll find:

Married?!	by Annette Broadrick
Designs on Love	by Gina Wilkins
It Happened One Night	by Marie Ferrarella
Lazarus Rising	by Anne Stuart

ADDED BONUS! In every edition of
Here Come the Grooms you'll find $5.00 worth
of coupons good for Harlequin and Silhouette
products.

On sale at your favorite Harlequin and Silhouette
retail outlet.

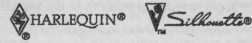 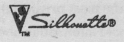

HARLEQUIN®   **Silhouette®**

You're About to Become a *Privileged* *Woman*

Reap the rewards of fabulous free gifts and benefits with proofs-of-purchase from Silhouette and Harlequin books

Pages & Privileges™

It's our way of thanking you for buying our books at your favorite retail stores.

✂

PROOF OF PURCHASE
SD-PP172
Offer expires October 31, 1996

**Harlequin and Silhouette—
the most privileged readers in the world!**

For more information about Harlequin and Silhouette's PAGES & PRIVILEGES program call the Pages & Privileges Benefits Desk: 1-503-794-2499

SD-PP172